Surrender

Published by Phaze Books

Cincinnati, Ohio

This is an explicit and erotic novel
intended for the enjoyment
of adult readers. Please keep
out of the hands of children.

www.Phaze.com

Surrender

Tales of Erotic Submission by

EDEN BRADLEY
ELIZA GAYLE
REESE GABRIEL
ALESSIA BRIO

A Phaze Production
Phaze Books
6470A Glenway Avenue, #109
Cincinnati, OH 45211-5222
Phaze is an imprint of Mundania Press, LLC.

To order additional copies of this book, contact:
books@phaze.com
www.Phaze.com

Edited by Robin Slick, Denise Jeffries, and Kathryn Lively

Trade Paperback ISBN-13: 978-1-59426-036-2

First Print Edition - June, 2008
Printed in the United States of America

10 9 8 7 6 5 4 3 2 1

Table of Contents

Breaking Skye
Eden Bradley

Also by Eden Bradley

Heat Wave

Chapter One

This could not be him. This man could not be the one who would strip her bare, put her on her knees and do unspeakable things to her…lovely, wicked things she had only ever imagined in the darkest corners of her mind.

When she'd posted the ad on bondage.com, she'd imagined finding a man with an air of command. A man who carried himself with utter confidence. A man who could guide her through this experience with capable hands.

He was all of these things. But he was too beautiful to be real. Like some fallen angel with his evil-looking goatee, his sharply honed bone structure, his too-lush mouth. He had shoulders like a Greek god beneath his black trench coat. Droplets of water clung to the fabric, and she watched as he shrugged out of the long coat and shivered a bit at the damp, San Francisco cold. Perhaps he was human after all.

He spoke her name in a low voice that felt like a caress. "Skye."

Certainty in his voice. She had a feeling this man never doubted himself. A Dominant through and through. What had she heard this kind of man called in her research on the Internet? A true Dominant?

"Yes. You must be Adam."

He nodded, took her hand as he slid into the chair across from hers. He held on just a moment too long, the flickering heat of his touch making her wonder if she wanted him to let go. The tiny café table seemed like too little space separating them. Adam Dunne had an enormous, palpable presence.

A waitress came as though summoned and took his order for an espresso while Skye made a brief study of his face. Absolutely masculine, every line, every plane. A short, thick thatch of brown hair a few shades lighter than his goatee. He had a small scar just below his lower lip, making his features appear even more masculine. His eyes were a dark, dusky blue, framed in thick lashes. God, what it would be like to have those eyes turned on her, focused...

She shivered and realized he still hadn't released her from his grip. She glanced down and saw another scar on the back of his left hand, a small crescent around the joint of the thumb. Why was it that she wanted to run her finger over it? When he turned to her, meeting her gaze, she shivered again with a fine, pure heat.

Lust.

She hadn't expected to feel this.

"Are you all right, Skye?" He smiled. Gorgeous white teeth.

All the better to eat you with.

She really had to get a hold of herself. Carry on a conversation like a normal person. She pulled her hand back and put it in her lap.

"What? Yes, I'm fine. Thank you."

"Am I the first Dominant you've contacted?"

"No. There have been several others, but they...I don't know. I wasn't comfortable with any of them."

"Are you comfortable with me?"

It felt like a trick question. Her pulse was racing at a thousand miles an hour.

"I don't know yet."

The waitress brought his espresso in a small, white china cup that looked even tinier in his hand as he lifted it and sipped.

"Just relax. We're here to get to know each other. To see if we'll work well together." He put his cup down and leaned forward a bit. "You said in your e-mail that you're interested in exploring what it's like to be a submissive. Interesting, the way you phrased it. It seemed detached. As though you don't think of yourself as a submissive."

Very observant. "I don't. I believe this is simply one small corner of myself. That this one experience will purge this...yearning from my system."

"I'm not sure that's a healthy attitude to have going in."

"I think exploring even your darkest side can be a healthy way to express repressed desires, needs. Once expressed, the need often disappears. It's the symbols that count, what these things represent to people. To me."

He sat back in his chair, raised one dark brow. "You truly believe that?"

"Of course. I'm an artist. I believe very strongly

in symbols."

"That's not what I meant. But you know that. Are you at all willing to have your mind changed?"

Why the sudden flutter in her stomach? She picked up the cup of Darjeeling tea she'd ordered before he'd arrived, sipped, found it cold. She set the cup down again.

He leaned forward in his chair until he was only inches from her. The warmth of his hand slid over hers again. He said quietly, "I think I can challenge your theory. But that's not why I want to do this with you. You intrigue me, Skye. I've worked as a trainer for ten years. I've learned to read people. I can read you. So strong on the outside. So controlled. You need to break that control. To let it go. I can do this for you. But only on my terms."

She swallowed hard. His hand on hers seemed to scorch her skin. Her whole body surged with need for his touch. She shook her head to clear it. "What exactly are you suggesting?"

"That you give yourself over to me."

"That's what I'd intended. For one night— "

"One night won't work. It'll take at least several evenings. This is a process, Skye, not an event. That's not how the human mind works. And as much as this experience will be physical, the most important part happens in your head. Brain chemistry, psychology, your personal history, symbols, as you said. It all comes into play. Did you really think you could do all that in one night?"

"I...I don't know..."

Her mind was spinning. She *had* thought that.

Foolish, she could see now. But could she do what he was suggesting? Losing control for one night, that she could manage. That she could excuse. But more?

He slid his hand up her arm, leaving a trail of sensation even through her cashmere sweater. When it came to rest on the bare skin at the back of her neck, her legs trembled and went weak. His hand was absolutely burning on her skin. Her body flooded with desire. Physical desire, yes. But also an inexplicable desire to please him. This stranger with the smoky blue eyes that seemed to see right through her. Eyes like the misty February sky outside.

Her heart hammered with panic. But she didn't want to run. She wanted—needed—to understand why this man was making her feel like some trembling virgin with starry-eyed fantasies flashing through her mind. The same images that had plagued her since she was a teenager. Fantasies she had finally decided to live out.

God, she was really going to do this!

He leaned in closer, until she felt the warmth of his coffee-scented breath on her cheek. "Say you want to, Skye."

"How...how much time?"

"As long as it takes."

God.

She licked her lips, tasted the faint peppermint of her lip gloss. "I understand your point, about needing more time. I'm just not sure..."

"Not sure you can do it?" he finished for her.

"Yes."

"There's only one way to find out."

He reached out and tilted her chin in his hand, forcing her to meet his dark blue gaze. His eyes were too intense. If he hadn't held her there, she would have looked away. Could he feel her shaking?

"Say you want to do this, Skye."

That velvet voice again, swarming over her like a soft blanket. Her whole body quivered with desire, just hearing his voice, feeling the sizzling heat of his fingertips on her chin, and those eyes…

She swallowed again, her mind fighting the sharp stab of need in her body. Her body was winning. "Yes. I want to do this."

* * * *

He'd thought for a moment she might change her mind. Those golden brown eyes like a doe's, the pupils enormous with nerves. Tiny, delicate bones to match. Too gorgeous, this woman. And smart. That always killed him. But he was here to do a job. A job he enjoyed, but a job nonetheless.

"We'll need to talk about a few things first."

She nodded. "Of course."

He could see from the faint movement of her long, brown hair that she was trembling. The sadist in him loved it. And hair like a dark curtain. He'd love to get his hands on it. In it. Pull it hard.

"Let's start with your name. Skye…?"

"Just Skye is fine."

Her tongue darted out, a flash of pink against the dusky rose of her plush, glossed lips, distracting him. Utterly kissable lips. But he was losing focus.

"We need to trust each other here."

She took in a deep breath, exhaled, played with her teacup. "It's Ballard. But it's my father's name. I don't use it."

"You can tell me why later. You said you're an artist? What medium?"

"It changes. Right now I love pen and ink, the starkness of it. And charcoal. I haven't been using any color lately, just exploring lines, shapes, contrast." She paused, looking uncertain. "I'm sorry. That was probably more than you wanted to know."

"On the contrary. I want to know. Everything. And I love the way your eyes light up talking about it. I love seeing the passion on your face."

She blushed, a pink sheen rising in her high, curved cheeks. He reached for her hand again and watched the blush deepen. He pulled it toward him, turned it over to inspect the tattoo curling around her left wrist, a small, sinuous piece done in dark, tribal style. He looked up at her, surprised, letting her hand go. "A phoenix?"

"Yes. It represents rebirth."

"I know. I have one, too."

"A tattoo?"

He nodded. "A phoenix."

A small laugh from her. "What a strange coincidence."

"I don't believe in coincidences. I'll show it to you eventually."

She nodded her head. Her nervousness radiated off her in waves, along with a subtle, smoky scent that made his cock harden. That was all right, she could be nervous. Should be, if she had any idea about what he planned to do to her. An image of her tied, naked, to his bed, and his cock sprang to life.

Yes, he had to get her there. He'd better get back on track.

"You've seen my references. I've read the list of desires you e-mailed to me, things you'd like to try: bondage, spanking, floggers, all of these things interest me, as well. We'll be a good match. I'm going to send you a questionnaire. There are a few things on there you probably hadn't thought about."

She was visibly shaking now. But he understood it was as much from excitement as from fear. Not that he minded if she was a little afraid. That only made it more exciting. Domination and submission, sadomasochism, were all about an energy exchange, after all. He fed off her energy. Pleasure, fright, it was all the same at that level. And this woman, as controlled as she tried to be, unconsciously wore her emotions on her sleeve. To play her would be fantastic. He couldn't wait to begin.

"I'll e-mail you as soon as I get home with the questionnaire. There will be some other things, instructions. Do you know about safe words?"

"Yes. I'm to use 'yellow' if I want to slow down a scene, if I can't handle something you're...doing, and 'red' if I need to stop completely."

"Exactly. Remember your safe words. Don't be embarrassed to use them. That's the only thing you're responsible for during play. I'll be responsible for everything else. You will be in my hands. Do you understand?"

She swallowed; he could see her throat working for a moment before she spoke. "Yes."

"I'll send you my address. Come Friday night."

She paused before nodding her head, looking for a moment as though she were going to argue. But in the end, she didn't question that he'd phrased it as a command. A momentary struggle. Enough that he could see she would fight yielding to him. But he had no doubt he could handle her. He'd trained girls like this before, those who had to hang on so tightly to control that letting it go was the ultimate relief. He loved nothing more than to break past that wall of reserve. The idea of breaking this particular girl, this beautiful woman whose very scent made him want to taste her skin, would be a pleasure. Hers. His.

Breaking Skye. He knew it was all he would think about all week.

Chapter Two

Skye let herself into her third-floor apartment, her hands still shaking. She hadn't been able to calm down since her conversation with Adam Dunne.

Had it really even happened? It all seemed dreamlike to her now. Too good to be true. Too frightening. But this was exactly what she'd wanted, wasn't it? And more. Too much more, maybe.

She'd wanted an experiment. An experience. But she hadn't expected to find a man—a Dominant—that she'd be so unbearably attracted to. That complicated things. And he was graceful in that way only utterly self-confident men could be. That was the sexiest thing about him. Except for his mouth, maybe...

She groaned and tossed her purse down on the antique sea chest in her front hall, kicked her shoes off and padded barefoot across the hardwood floors of her small living room to the bay window overlooking the city.

The apartment was on a hill overlooking the Castro district. This was a beautiful neighborhood: well-kept, safe. And one of the few areas in San Francisco to get the occasional bit of sun.

It was twilight now, and the evening fog was rolling in, turning the lights on the streets below her into a glowing wash of color. Wisps of fog threaded its way between the mini-Tudors and remodeled Victorians that lined the streets. Cold and lonely-looking out there, as San Francisco often was. But she was glad for the sense of solitude now. She had a lot to think about.

Had she gotten in over her head here? Her whole body gave a long shiver as she pictured Adam in her mind. He obviously knew exactly what he was doing. She felt so...naïve. Yet he obviously didn't expect anything more from her.

I'll be responsible for everything...

Yes, she knew he would be, had an absolute sense of that. How frightening. How freeing.

She had three days to ponder this, to look over the questionnaire he would send her, to make her final decision. He'd already assumed she would come to him, but she had to really think this over, now that she'd met him, didn't she?

Her heart surged in her chest, her limbs going warm and weak as she imagined his face. Oh, hell, who was she kidding? She'd made her decision the moment she'd seen him walk into the café. She wanted this. More specifically, she wanted to do these things with him. In fact, if she were going to be perfectly honest, she could hardly wait to see him again. Three days suddenly seemed like far too long to wait.

* * * *

Wednesday and Thursday had passed quickly enough; she taught a few art classes at the local junior college, which kept her busy and distracted. But she'd spent her evenings going over and over the long questionnaire Adam had sent her.

He was right, there were things on there that had never occurred to her. Some of them too scary to contemplate, some of them enticing. Would she like to play with hot wax? Maybe. Would she like to try caning? She just might. Would she allow any sexual contact?

Her mind had emptied as she read that question, her body flooding with hot desire.

Oh, yes...

Since then, her head had been filled with images of him touching her. She'd spent most of Thursday night in bed with her collection of vibrators. But orgasm after orgasm didn't satisfy her. She had to feel his touch, she knew, before the aching desire that ran hot through her veins would be sated.

Friday morning, she awoke with that same need humming through her system, but she resisted, wanting to save it all for him, to go to him with this almost unbearable wanting. A sort of torture, she thought, loving the idea.

She spent the day preparing, allowing herself to think of him, indulging herself, really. Her body was nearly throbbing by evening, when she laid out her clothes on her old iron bed, the outfit he had requested: a short, black skirt; a white button-down blouse; sheer, black, thigh-high stockings; high black pumps. She wore nothing underneath, making her feel sexy, a little vulnerable, a lot wicked.

She bathed herself, careful not to give in to the need to slide her fingers over her aching pussy, her swollen nipples, as she leaned against the cool, white tiles in the shower. The contrast of the hot water and the tiles at her back was a surprisingly erotic sensation. When she got out and dried herself off, she rubbed scented lotion into her skin, every touch of her own hands an unexpectedly sensual experience.

How much better would it be when she stood before him?

Finally it was time to go, and she called for a cab. The ride over to his house in Noe Valley seemed to take forever. It was one of those classic 1920s stucco homes that were so popular in the city: three stories, with the garage on the ground floor, a small iron railing balcony at each window. She got out of the cab and walked up the stairs on one side of the garage to the front door. It stood silent sentry, daring her to knock. Why did she feel as though her life was about to change forever?

Because it is.

She took a deep breath and ordered her racing pulse to calm. It didn't help.

She knocked anyway.

And felt the breath escaping her lungs when Adam opened the door.

So damn handsome. No, that word was not enough. He was stunning, in his black slacks, his white shirt rolled up at the sleeves. Flash of strong, white teeth as he smiled at her. Flash of burning lust when he took her hand and guided her inside.

"Welcome, Skye."

"Thank you." She didn't know what else to say, feeling shy suddenly. Overwhelmed. And something else, something to do with being in his presence. She didn't understand it. It felt good, right, yet she almost wanted to cry at the same time.

"Come and have a seat on the sofa."

He led her into the living room. Beautiful house, great architectural details. Her artist's eye took it all in quickly: the scrolling crown molding, the polished wood floors, the gorgeous mantle. All white walls, an eclectic collection of contemporary and antique furnishings. The enormous beige sofa was all clean, modern lines, while the square coffee table was a gorgeously carved piece of old Indonesian teak topped in glass. Soothing, neutral colors everywhere, except for the really astonishing art on the walls and the dark red Persian rugs on the floors.

She sat on the sofa, her stomach fluttering, unsure as to what to do with her hands. She fisted them at her sides, finally. Her stomach gave a sharp jump when he sat down beside her.

"You don't need to be nervous," he said quietly. "But I don't mind if you are."

Another smile, this one definitely wicked. She averted her gaze. But he immediately cupped her chin in his hand, forcing her to look into those dusky blue eyes.

His voice was more commanding this time. "Don't hide your eyes from me again." He was quiet a moment, allowing her to absorb his words. "The eyes really are the windows to the soul. And I need to know you on the inside if this is going to work. Understood?"

"Yes. I just...something is happening to me already..." She shook her head helplessly.

"I can see that. And trust me, it's good. You're responding to the mere idea of what we're about to do. I can only imagine how you'll respond once we begin. Do you have any questions?"

"I...don't know. When do we begin? Is it now?"

That devastating smile again. "Yes."

He stood, offered her his hand. She took it, let him guide her to her feet.

A small wave of panic hit her. "Where are we going?"

He turned to her, and she realized she'd never been this close to him before. He seemed even taller, standing right next to her. He smelled like pure male. Just clean skin and a hint of earthy musk. Sexy as hell.

"Shh, no more questions now. No speaking unless you're spoken to, or unless it's to use your safe words." He cupped her face in his palm, making her legs go weak with desire and something else, that sensation she couldn't seem to put a name to. "You are in my hands now, Skye. No more worries, no concerns, no control here. I will do it all. For you. Just let it go. That's why you're here."

"I...I'm not sure if I can."

"You can. And you will. For me."

She nodded, unable to speak. Yes. For him. She wanted nothing else at this moment. What was happening to her? She couldn't think clearly enough to figure it out.

When he quietly ordered her to undress, the breath went right out of her.

"Wh—what?"

"I said to take your clothes off." His voice was low but certain.

Tears threatened, but she bit her lip and held them back.

He stood before her. She was shaking her head again, unable to speak. He pulled her right up against him, and his scent went through her like a small storm of sensation. Dizzying. Electrifying, with his big body warm against her and his breath in her hair.

"Skye, listen to me. You are going to have to find a way to do as I tell you. To accept that. To yield. As I said before, this is a process. If you can't give yourself over to the process, we can't do this. But I think you can. I know you can. I see that in you. Cry if you need to. It doesn't matter. All that matters is just doing it. Do you understand what I'm saying?"

She nodded, squeezing her eyes shut. She wanted to do what he told her to, but she was so damn scared suddenly.

"It's too real," she whispered.

"Too real to deal with?"

"No, just...incredibly, intensely real."

"Tell me again that you want to be here."

"I do, I swear it." She pulled back and looked up at him then, caught his blue gaze. Was struck again by his pure, male beauty. Yes, every cell in her being wanted to be here.

"Just stop thinking," he told her.

How could he know that was exactly what she was doing? "I'm trying."

"Come with me. I'll help you."

He took her hand and led her across the room. She followed blindly down a long hall, through a doorway, into a dimly lit space. When she finally allowed herself to look around her, she saw an enormous, four-poster bed, an overstuffed chair with a large ottoman covered in suede, a fireplace with a high mantle. A fire was burning, the acrid scent flooding her nostrils, the amber glow casting the only light in the room.

He took her to the chair and sat down, pulled her so she stood before him. Silently, he unbuttoned her blouse, his hands gentle, almost tender. She was trembling all over, with fear, with excitement, with an exquisite anticipation she'd never felt before. When he pulled her blouse from her shoulders, her nipples went hard beneath the intensity of his gaze.

"Beautiful," he murmured.

She could not believe she was standing here, allowing this man, this virtual stranger, to undress her. That she stood so silently, so passively. Yet at the same time, it was her very passiveness that allowed her to do it.

When he unzipped her skirt and let it slide down her thighs, she gasped.

"Shh," he soothed. "Relax."

But how could she relax when she wanted so desperately for him to touch her? Her mind was spinning with the possibilities. Something about his touch, the way his eyes roved over her almost reverently, was causing a strange sort of heaviness in her limbs. And the vee between her thighs grew damper every moment.

And then he put his hands on her. Just laid his fingertips against the skin on the front of her thighs. That touch went through her like an electric current, sending a stab of excitement straight to her sex. She was shaking as he stroked her skin with small, feather-like touches. He moved his hands higher, and she took in a deep breath.

When he slid his hands to the back of her thighs and squeezed hard enough to hurt, she gasped. But she didn't move.

"Good girl. Very good."

Something about the pleasure in his voice made her heart surge. And the words themselves. *Good girl.* Lovely.

He spent some time just running his hands over her, tracing the curves of her body. His touch left a trail of sensation everywhere. Her body was heating up beneath his hands, her sex growing heavy with need, her breasts full and aching.

"That's it," he said. "Enjoy this, being touched. Close your eyes. Let it happen."

She did as he said, closing her eyes, letting her head fall back as he continued to brush her skin with his fingertips: her thighs, her stomach, the back of her hands. Soon she wanted to beg him to touch her breasts, to slip a hand between her thighs. Her sex was pulsing. Every inch of her body seemed to have a direct connection, sending currents of excitement coursing through her.

When he finally swept his fingers across her

already hard nipples, she gasped aloud and opened her eyes. She found him staring up at her, amusement in those hazy blue eyes. But something else, as well. Lust? Yes. He was as excited as she was. And that knowledge made her soar with a sense of power she didn't quite understand. But then he took her nipples between his fingers, pinching lightly, and she couldn't think any more. Her mind was simply telling her, *yes, more...*

He tugged and rolled her nipples, paused to cup the weight of her breasts in his hands, went back to pinch her again. God, it felt good, like something she'd needed all her life. Her secret desire.

A sharp flash of heat when he said, "Spread your legs for me, Skye."

She did as he asked instantly. She felt open, exposed. He moved in until his face was only inches from her body, and she could feel the heat of his breath on her belly. She had never felt so naked. So vulnerable. So turned on.

He took in a deep breath and said, "You smell like heaven, Skye."

Then he brushed her mound with one hand, just a brief, feathering touch, and she thought she'd fall over. Desire rushed through her, ran hot in her veins like a fiery tide. She moaned.

"I can feel your need, Skye. I can smell it on you. Trust that I will feed it tonight. I will satisfy your cravings in a way you've never experienced before."

She loved the command in his tone. Loved the husky edge of raw desire even more.

"I'm going to turn you over my knee now. I'm going to spank you."

He pulled her toward him, but she fought him, struggling against a wave of panic. Over his knee? That seemed so…personal. Intimate. Could she really lie naked over his lap, with him fully clothed and in control of the situation? Her heart thudded a heavy rhythm in her chest, making it hard to breathe. Could she give that much power to another person? Could she allow herself to be so entirely vulnerable?

"I…I can't. Adam, I can't do this."

Chapter Three

Adam snaked his hand up and gripped the back of her neck, forced her down to her knees on the floor in front of him. He buried his hand in her hair, pulled her head back so she had no choice but to look into his face. It hurt. Tears stung her eyes. Her pulse raced. A flood of damp heat pooled between her thighs.

"You will do as I say, Skye. You will obey. Do you understand me?"

She nodded her head as much as she could with him still holding her so tightly. His face was stern, but there was no anger there. Why did she find that reassuring?

His voice went softer. "I understand what you're going through. When you truly give yourself over to this, to *me*, the panic will go away. And what I'm about to do will help you."

He pulled her up and into his lap, turned her face down. The wool of his slacks was scratchy against her stomach, the front of her thighs. He smoothed his palms over her back as he talked to her, helping her to handle it, to accept what was happening.

"You need this, Skye. You need a little pain to

give you the chemical release in your brain that will make this all good for you. Endorphins. You got a little just from me touching you. You're so damn responsive."

A small pinch at the skin on the underside of her buttocks, making her wince. But it didn't hurt, she realized.

He went on, his voice growing deeper, smokier. "You have a gorgeous body. Your skin is incredible, flawless."

He drew one finger slowly down the length of her spine, causing a ripple of desire to dance over her flesh. When he got to her buttocks, he moved lower, dipping between her thighs, brushing her pussy lips. She squirmed, parted her legs a bit more.

"Good girl. You like it, don't you? You'll love it all, I promise. I'll see to it."

The first slap was nothing more than a quick rap against her skin. Sensation more than pain. He began a slow rhythm, moving his hands over her buttocks. She was surprised that, while there was a slow build of pain as he increased the tempo and force, it felt good. And the harder he smacked her, the wetter her sex grew.

"Breathe into it, Skye, into the pain, into the pleasure."

The spanking went on, harder and harder. Tremors of pleasure moved over her skin, spread over her body in rolling waves. She felt an odd sinking sensation and understood what it was she'd experienced when she'd first met him. Her mind was letting go, moving to some other plane. Here, she was hyperaware. She could feel the hard muscles of his thighs beneath her, her breasts crushed into his lap. And the solid ridge of his erection against her belly. She moved her hips, grinding into him.

"Hold still."

She tried. But as the volley of smacks rained down on her, her flesh heating up, it became almost impossible.

When he moved a hand between her thighs and plunged two fingers right into her wet, aching heat, she jumped.

"Shhh," he soothed her, pressing down on the small of her back. "Tell me, Skye, do you need to come?"

"Yes!"

"I'll make you come. But not yet."

She wanted to cry. But she bit her lip, did her best to be compliant. Wondered for a moment that she found herself wanting that, to obey his orders. To please him.

He started to spank her again, kept his fingers in her wet, needy pussy. She wanted to beg him to pump into her. She clenched her jaw to keep quiet. And frankly, his hand slapping her ass felt almost as good to her as his fingers inside her. She didn't understand, didn't try to.

The slaps grew harder, sharp and stinging. Her skin was on fire. And her pussy burned with the most exquisite need she'd ever experienced. Harder, faster, until the pain reverberated through her body, inside and out. The shock wave of that alone caused spearing shafts of pleasure in her sex, in her breasts, all over her.

He moved his fingers deeper, and the first wave of climax caused her to clench around them.

"Not yet."

She squeezed her eyes shut and commanded her body to calm. He held perfectly still, until she had herself under control. Then, as though he knew she was ready for more, he smacked her ass hard, then harder, and pumped her with his fingers.

She whimpered, couldn't control the sound.

"Soon," he told her, still working her with his fingers, still smacking her ass.

Then a sharp volley of hard, punishing slaps, making her wince. Pain coursed through her. When he pressed onto her clit with his thumb, pleasure joined the pain, became one sensation. She came apart under his hands.

Her orgasm slammed into her like a brick wall. Pleasure, pain shafted through her. Her sex pulsed, clenched. Behind her eyes was an explosion of white light, and she was blinded by pure sensation, by the raw power of it.

She knew she yelled. She didn't care.

He worked her mercilessly, milking her orgasm for all it was worth, until she was squirming and moaning in his lap. Totally out of control. Undone.

When it was over, he was quiet, but she could hear the ragged cadence of his breath. His cock was still rock-hard beneath her. She wanted him inside of her body, even now.

He pulled her up so she was sitting in his lap, his arms around her. He took her chin in his hand, searched her eyes. "You are fucking beautiful, Skye. Like nothing I've ever seen before."

A warm glow filled her at his words, the reverent tone of his voice.

"And you take it well. Your body soaks it up. Revels in it." He spoke in a quiet mutter, almost as though he spoke only to himself. "Have to try some other things with you, but later. Later. You're done for now."

He stood with her in his arms and carried her to the bed, laid her down and draped a blanket over her.

"I'll bring you something to drink," he told her before walking from the room.

She was fine lying there, drowsing, not allowing herself to dissect what had happened to her. She wanted to simply feel for a while, to bask in this druglike haze. She could easily become addicted to this.

No, she wasn't thinking clearly. This was temporary. But she couldn't really think it through at the moment. Too sleepy. Too happy to be there, with him. *Adam.* Right now, there was nothing more in the world she wanted.

* * * *

What the hell was wrong with him? Adam paced his narrow kitchen, a glass of water in his hand. He should bring it to her. But he needed a minute to calm down.

Christ, the way she squirmed and moaned in his lap…

He'd spanked dozens of other beautiful women. But none had ever affected him the way

Skye did. What was it about her? Maybe the way she'd fought so hard when they were talking about it, then slipped into it as easily as any experienced submissive the moment he laid his hands on her?

Whatever it was, he had the hard-on of his life, and he'd been seconds from tearing his clothes off and fucking her senseless.

Unforgivable, that loss of control for a Dom.

Even now, he couldn't get the image of her rounded ass, her skin pinking beautifully under his hands, out of his mind. That glorious mass of chestnut hair falling over the naked skin of her back. Fucking poetry, everything about this woman.

He had to get back in there. Inexcusable to leave her alone after her first play session. He had to pull himself together.

He ran a hand through his hair, dragged in a long breath, blew it out, and headed back to the bedroom. She was draped across his bed, her pose languorous, utterly relaxed. The blanket he'd wrapped her in had fallen, exposing one perfect breast. Unbelievable, that gorgeous skin, the areola a dusky pink, her darker pink nipple swollen and so damn succulent all he wanted was to take it in his mouth…

Instead he bent over her, helped her to sit up and take a few sips of water.

"How are you?"

"Fine. Great, if you really want to know." She smiled, dazzling him. Too beautiful.

"I'll keep you here a while, let you come down, before I take you home."

"Home? Do I have to go?"

Her voice was a soft, husky sound. Hell, he'd keep her here forever, if he could.

But of course, he couldn't do that.

"Don't worry. You'll be here with me a while."

"Okay." The answer seemed to satisfy her. She closed her eyes, her dark lashes lying like a sooty fringe against her flushed cheeks.

He sat down on the bed, avoiding touching her. His cock was as hard as it had ever been. He was still rock-hard an hour later when he helped her get dressed, put her in his car and drove her home.

She was quiet in the car as they sped through the dark city. He was grateful for her lambent sleepiness. Grateful he didn't have to make conversation. His head was too twisted up.

The point was driven further home when they arrived at her building and he had to help her from the car and up the stairs, her warm little body pressed against him all the way. The scent of her, the feel of her, was making his stomach tighten up.

He got her inside the apartment, quickly took in the comfortable furnishings, the beautifully worn antiques. He took her coat from her shoulders, sat her down on the overstuffed velvet sofa. Her long hair was mussed, her eyes glazed, her lips a perfect cherry red, wanting to be kissed. But all he dared was a quick brush of his mouth across hers.

"You'll be fine," he told her. He didn't dare linger. He was too undone. He didn't trust himself.

"Yes, I'm fine. Wonderful. A little tired." She smiled sleepily.

"Okay. I'm going to let you get some rest then. I'll see you later."

He made his escape—for that's exactly what it was—as quickly as he could down the old staircase, and onto the street. He got in his car, started the engine and drove home a little too fast.

Back at his place, he spent the rest of the night pacing his living room, trying to figure out what was wrong with him. Why he could barely stand to leave her at her apartment despite the driving need to flee.

He never became attached to a woman. Never had, never would. He understood why he was like this, the lone wolf. He had damn good reason to be. He'd had one huge loss early in life, and he wasn't about to set himself up to go through that again. Ever. He'd successfully avoided attachment since that god-awful night, so long ago. So why was it so damn hard to let Skye go?

He strode to the sideboard in his dining room, poured himself a scotch and threw it back. It burned going down, a cleansing burn. He poured himself another.

He was supposed to see her next Friday. He'd better have his shit together by then. He would. Control was key. The antithesis of weakness. He'd had years of practice. He knew how to do it, how to keep his emotions at bay.

The problem was that he'd never been challenged in quite this way before. While he told himself he could handle this situation, he wasn't quite sure he believed it.

* * * *

Morning dawned with the usual San Francisco fog floating outside her bedroom windows. Skye glanced at the clock on her nightstand. Almost ten. Late for her. But she didn't want to get out of her warm bed yet. She stretched, noticing how her arms and legs felt used, a little sore. She ran a hand over her bottom and smiled at the tenderness of the skin there.

Why should this make her happy?

She didn't know. She only knew that it did.

She smoothed her hands over her body: her stomach, her ribs, her breasts. Beneath her fingertips, her nipples came up hard. Her skin was hypersensitive everywhere, as though her night with Adam had awoken something in her.

She wasn't thrilled that he'd been right about her. She was too much attached to her own sense of control to be happy about that. But she couldn't deny the way her body had responded to the things Adam had done to her. Hell, she couldn't deny what it had done to her head.

And maybe to her heart.

But no, that was ridiculous. She hardly knew the man.

I know everything I need to know.

Why was the voice in her head so damn smug? Maybe because it was right? But what did she really know? He was gorgeous, intelligent, articulate. He was kinky. But no, that wasn't quite right. Adam was a true sensualist. She could see it in everything he did. The way he moved, the way he touched her, in the simple, sensuous luxury of his home. The perfect man for her, really. Except that this BDSM thing was a huge part of his life, and for her, it was a temporary experience. All they had was a little time together, a few days, perhaps a few weeks. By then, she would have this urge out of her system, and whatever was going on between them would be over. Just as it was supposed to be.

And he certainly hadn't given her any hint that this would continue longer than was necessary for her to understand what her desires were all about. Hell, they hadn't even slept together. What reason would he have to become attached to her? And why did she want him to be?

Tears stung her eyes, just thinking about how he'd stayed next to her on the bed after he'd spanked her last night. Just sat with her, stroking her hair. What kind of man did that? Then he'd dressed her, taken her home. Every moment, every gesture, had been gentle, caring.

He was just doing his job.

Yes, of course. It was that irrational, girlish part of her that thought she'd read something more there. A part of her she'd closed off a long time ago.

It seemed Adam Dunne was loosening the tight hold she'd always kept over her emotions. Opening her up. Breaking her open. He frankly scared the hell out of her. But she would go back to him next Friday night.

She wouldn't miss it for all the world.

Chapter Four

She rode the same route in the cab to Adam's house she had the week before, but she felt completely different. This time she had some idea of what might happen there. She knew the scent of him, the feel of his hands on her skin. She was soaking wet by the time she reached his door.

He'd made her wait the week, to give her time to think. To figure out if this was working for her. To be certain that this was what she truly wanted.

She'd never wanted anything so much in her life.

The week had been pure torture. Adam had called her a couple of times. Friendly conversations, about work, the usual things people talked about who were getting to know one another. She'd found out what a huge art fan he was, that he played hockey on the weekends. Such normal activities for such an unusual man.

When she got to his house and he answered his door, he was just as absurdly handsome as he'd been before. He seemed more deliciously imposing tonight as he smiled wickedly, turned and led her into the dining room this time. He was dressed all in black. The color of sin.

The lighting in the house was dim, but she could still see the carved legs of the antique dining table. All of the chairs had been pulled away to ring the edge of the room. No artwork, just enormous, ornately framed mirrors on every wall. On a heavy, antique sideboard, tall silver candelabras held ivory tapers, the flames making their shadows dance.

He turned to her. "Take your clothes off, Skye. And get on the table."

He reached out and slid his hand around the back of her neck, heating her skin up instantly. Her body filled with the aching need to please him. She began to remove her clothing, her hands shaking. Her mind emptied out, allowing her to let go. With the last shred of reason, she realized it was Adam's mere presence that was doing this to her head.

Soon she was naked, and he smiled down at her, his smoky blue eyes glittering. He moved in closer, until she could feel the heat emanating from him. The faint, male scent of him was making her dizzy. She closed her eyes.

"Get up on the table now, Skye. Come, I'll help you."

He took her hand, steadied her while she climbed onto the cool, wood surface.

"Lie on your back," he told her, pushing her down just enough for her to understand completely that he was in control.

The table was hard and silky at the same time. And she felt as naked as she ever had in her life. Naked and strangely beautiful. Even more so when Adam began to run his hands over her body: her stomach, her thighs, her arms. They finally closed around her wrists, locking them into a pair of padded leather cuffs.

She gasped.

"It's all right, Skye. Trust me. The binding will only free you more."

By the time he'd cuffed both wrists and ankles, her heart was racing. But the vee between her thighs was soaked and pulsing with need. She pulled on the cuffs, testing them. He must have cuffed her to the table legs somehow. She couldn't move, her arms and legs spread wide. She loved it.

He stood over her, stroking her skin again, his touch lighting tiny fires of desire all over her. When he took her nipples between his fingers and rolled them, she sighed with pleasure. When he pinched them hard, she moaned in pain. But it all felt good. He kept at it, tugging, pinching. Sensation shot through her body, her sex. She wished he would use those clever fingers between her legs.

Please...

He gathered her breasts in his hands, pushing them together.

"Too damn perfect," he muttered. Then he let her go and turned away.

She had one small moment of panic simply because he was no longer touching her. But soon he turned back to her, leaned in close to her face and told her, "Stay as still as you can, Skye. This is going to hurt."

* * * *

He watched her pupils widen at his threatening words, exactly the effect he'd been after. Not that it was a lie, of course. This *was* going to hurt.

He pulled from his pocket a tiny, red, plastic clothespin he'd picked up at a crafts store. Amazing the things one could find there. Or in a supermarket, a hardware store. Pervertibles, he liked to call them, these everyday objects that could so easily be turned into instruments of torture.

Leaning over Skye's bound body, he smoothed a few fingers over the soft skin at the edge of her left breast. An exquisitely sensitive area, he knew. He pinched the skin together lightly between his fingers, pulled a bit, and fastened the tiny clothespin there. He smiled when she sucked in a sharp breath.

"Breathe into it, Skye. It'll get a bit worse before it gets better. I'm going to put a lot more of these on you."

He pulled a few more of the pins from his pocket, and created a small arc of them down the side of her breast. Every pin caused a small, satisfying gasp. He loved the sound of it, that whisper-soft noise coming from between her plump, red lips. And Christ, those lips...all he could think of when he looked at her mouth was pushing his cock in, fucking that lush mouth. His cock filled, hardened.

Control.

Yes, he needed to control himself. He'd thought this would be easier, without her hot little body pressed against him. But it didn't seem to matter. Just looking at her was challenging his self-control.

Focus.

He moved in again and began a line of the wicked little pins down the side of her right breast. By the time he was done, she was panting hard. He stepped back to look at his handiwork.

"Beautiful."

And she was. So fucking beautiful he could hardly stand to look at her. Bound to the table, her legs spread wide so that he could see her pink pussy lips, damp and inviting as hell. And the pins pinching her skin. He knew it hurt, could see it in the dilation of her pupils, in the sharp cadence of her breath. He wanted to hurt her. He wanted to bring her pleasure. He wanted to do everything to her. For her.

He slipped a hand between her thighs and right into the heat of her. Like hot silk inside. What would his cock feel like wrapped up in that slippery heat?

He pumped his fingers into her, pressed onto her hard little clit with his thumb, making her squirm. Then he pulled the first pin off.

She yelped.

"Yes, I know it hurts, worse coming off than going on. The blood is rushing back into your skin. I know how bad it is, but it's good at the same time, isn't it, Skye?"

"Yes..." She groaned, her head thrashing from side to side.

"You can handle it. I promise you." He leaned in and brushed a kiss over her hot cheek. "It's about to get much worse."

He pulled another pin off, and this time, rather than waiting for her to ride the pain out, immediately pulled off two more. She arched up off the table. He plunged his fingers deep into her pussy.

"Oh!"

"Yes, pain and pleasure, all at the same time." He caught her face in his free hand, held her chin, forcing her to look at him. Her golden brown eyes were glowing. "You love it, don't you, Skye? Tell me you want more."

"Yes...," she panted. "Please, Adam."

The pant turned into a whimpering cry when he circled her clit with his thumb, pressing down. He took another pin off.

"Oh...oh, oh, oh..."

He pumped his fingers into her, removed the last few pins in rapid succession. She was crying out, over and over, her sex clenching around his fingers. And as she came into his hand, he leaned in and crushed his mouth to hers. He needed her so damn much at that moment. Needed her to come into his mouth, to drink in her breath, to taste the sweetness of her. She thrashed beneath him, as much as she was able to in her tight bonds. His cock was so hard he thought he might burst. He thrust his tongue into her hot little mouth, pumped into her tight, clasping pussy with his fingers. And almost broke apart as she came and came.

* * * *

It seemed like forever before she was able to catch her breath. And Adam kept kissing her: tiny, hot kisses over her cheeks, her lips, her eyelids. When she was finally able to open her eyes and look at him, his whole expression was soft, somehow. His eyes were dark and glittering, his mouth as bruised-looking as she knew her own must be. He frankly looked undone. Shocking, to see him like this.

Her heart surged. And all she wanted was to be in his arms.

"Adam..."

He looked at her almost helplessly, shaking his head. "If I uncuff you now, Skye, I am bound to do something I'll regret, and maybe you will, too." He paused, ran a hand back over his hair. "Fuck me, but I am barely hanging on right now."

"Don't hang on. Let it go, Adam, as I have. I need you."

How was she able to even put a coherent sentence together? She pulled hard against her bonds. "Please," she begged.

"Fuck, fuck, fuck," he muttered, unbuckling the cuffs from her wrists, massaging them, then doing the same with her ankles. As soon as he leaned over her to ask if she was okay, she wrapped her arms around his neck and pulled him down, planting a firm kiss on his mouth.

He pulled back. The look on his face was pure shock, and she wondered for a moment if he might be angry with her. Then his whole expression shifted, his eyes going glassy, color rising in his cheeks.

"God damn it. Damn me," he murmured before he grabbed her face in his hands and kissed her.

His mouth came down hard on hers. Brutal, crushing. But his lips were soft and warm. His mouth was even softer when he opened hers and his tongue drove inside. His kiss was pure animal need. Frantic. She held on while he bruised her with his lips, while they panted into each others' mouths. It was as though they were one singular, driving need.

Without taking his mouth from her, he stripped his shirt off, then his pants. In a moment he was on top of her, skin to skin. The weight of his body was the most erotic sensation she'd ever experienced. She had never needed anything more. Her legs went around his wide back, and she felt the ridge of a long scar under the tender skin of her left thigh, where it pressed against the side of his ribcage. But she forgot all about it when his thick cock probed at the opening between her thighs. And he was kissing her and kissing her, until she couldn't breathe, couldn't think. All she knew was the feel and the scent of him. *Adam*.

They were moving together, their hips grinding, his cock pressing against her mound, burning hot. Her body shook with need, with the pure pleasure of him on top of her, the wet heat of his tongue in her mouth. She needed to come again.

When he shifted and slid the head of his cock into her, her sex clamped hard around him. God, he was big. His cock was a hot, pulsing shaft, paused at the entrance of her needy sex.

He pulled his mouth from hers, looked down into her face. Then, with his gaze locked on hers, he plunged inside.

She was filled, stretched, hurting and delirious with pleasure at the same time. The pleasure shot through her system like wildfire. Her clit pulsed, on the edge of climax already. She didn't think it could get any better until he pulled back, then drove into her body. Her hips moved to meet his. He pulled out, pushed into her again, and again she met his thrust. They moved in a primal rhythm, sensation driving through her, a powerful force. She could do nothing but give in to it.

The pressure built along with the pleasure. He bent his head to bite at her neck, his teeth sharp. She gloried in the pain, in the sensation of him marking her. Yes, pure animal. But she was no more than that as she raked her nails down his back, dug in as the first wave of her climax slammed into her. Her pussy was on fire, his cock pounding into her over and over. And she shattered beneath him, exploding with a molten rush of liquid heat.

The scent of him in her nostrils, the feel of his big body crushing her, it was all part of it. And she was coming and coming. He didn't stop, even when his own climax made every muscle in his body go rigid. He twisted his hands in her hair, and the sound that came out of him was a guttural growl. Still he pumped into her, until she was weak and shivering beneath him.

When he finally stopped, she couldn't move. Her arms were still around his neck, her legs wrapped around him. His cock was still hard inside her. His face was buried in her neck, his breath hot against her skin. She wanted to stay just like that forever. Never wanted him to let her go.

At that thought, her chest tightened, and the damn tears wanted to start again. She bit down on her lip, trying to hold them back. But she couldn't do it. A sob broke through before she could prevent it.

"Ah, damn it, Skye."

Chapter Five

Adam raised his head, looked into her eyes, and saw they were brimming with emotion as much as they were with tears. The sight of her like this hit him like a blow to the chest. "Skye, I don't mean it like that. I'm not angry. Not with you. I'm angry with myself. I should never have done this to you."

He stroked her cheek, and she turned her face into his palm, closing her eyes. Skin like hot satin. His hand was wet with her tears. *Shit.* "This is exactly why I never should have done this."

"I wanted you to," she whispered, her voice rough. "I begged you."

"Still, it was my responsibility to stay in control. But I lose it when I'm with you, Skye. You just... shatter me."

Christ, had he really said that out loud?

He wiped at her tears with his thumbs. "I'm sorry."

"Please don't be. Don't tell me you're sorry about any of this!"

"Fuck," he muttered, then gathered her in his arms, and carried her into the living room. He laid her down on the sofa, draped a blanket over her, and sat next to her, naked still. His heart was hammering. Pure panic. What the hell was going on with him? And Christ, she was beautiful. He'd never seen such a purely beautiful being in his life. But right now, she looked absolutely tortured. His gut twisted with guilt.

She stared up at him for a few moments. "Adam, tell me why this was so wrong. Haven't you ever slept with the girls you trained before?"

"Of course."

"And I did say on the questionnaire you gave me that sexual contact was fine."

"Yes."

"Then why?"

He raked a hand back over his hair once more. *Keep it simple.* "I don't get emotionally involved with the girls I train."

"Who do you become emotionally involved with?" she asked, her voice quiet.

"No one."

"I see." She paused. "But this was sex. I wasn't asking for anything more. So why was it wrong?"

"You weren't asking for anything more? Christ, Skye, every look you give me, every response to my touch, is asking for more."

The tears started again in her big, brown eyes, and again guilt washed over him. "Look, I'm not saying that's wrong. It's me. *I'm* all wrong."

"You feel right to me. Is that...an illusion? Maybe I made it all up, because of what...because of the things we're doing together. Because of the intensity."

He had to stop and think about that. A lot of

new submissives became attached to the people who played them well. But it did nothing to explain what was going on with him, why he hadn't been able to maintain the carefully held control he'd developed over the years he'd been involved in the BDSM lifestyle. He'd held himself back from having sex with Skye because he'd been aware from the first moment he'd seen her that he could easily lose control. The attraction had been too strong—insanely strong. So, why hadn't he just turned away?

Because he'd *had* to have her, touch her, make her his.

He was in big fucking trouble.

Even more so when she asked him, "What do you think made you this way? What is it that shuts you off from becoming emotionally involved? And I think, regardless of what you're saying, you're not completely shut off. If you were, you would have maintained control, wouldn't you?" She paused, bit her lip. "I know you don't want to hear this. And I don't know whether to be flattered or angry that it's happened with me. Because it's so…it makes it so much harder for me to keep any emotional distance at all, these tempting glimpses of what you have to offer, if only you'd let yourself."

She was right. But this was exactly the sort of thing he could not deal with.

"I can't explain myself to you, Skye."

"Meaning you won't."

Her mouth set in a stubborn line. He had to respect that in her, that she would argue with him like this.

She sat up, leaned in toward him, and he could smell her. Her faint, smoky perfume, the scent of her arousal, the musk of sex. That leftover fragrance of him fucking her on the table. But it hadn't just been fucking for him, had it? That's what was freaking him out. Not that he'd done it, but his reaction to it. To her.

"Tell me, Adam. Tell me why."

He shook his head. He didn't talk to anyone about his past, about the things that had made him shut down. She was right about that. But he'd never discussed what he'd been through with anyone. Why did he want to tell her about it suddenly? Nothing was making sense anymore.

Skye reached out and laid her soft hand on his arm, said quietly, "Tell me."

He drew in a long breath, blew it out. Was he really going to talk to her about this? Even as the battle raged in his mind, he said, "There was an accident."

She just nodded, but he couldn't believe he'd said the words aloud. The rest wanted to come pouring out, as though through a crack in a dam.

"It was a long time ago. I was fifteen. My older sister, Beth, had picked me up from a party. It was late. I was drunk. I'd called her to come and get me and my best friend, Clay." His heart was thundering like a freight train in his chest, but he made himself spit the rest out. "We were hit by a drunk driver. And she...Beth and Clay both died that night. But not me. I'll never know why I'm still here. Fuck, that sounds pathetic, doesn't it? So, yeah, I shut a part of myself down after that. A normal reaction, I'm told."

"It is." Skye stroked her fingertips down his arm. "But it's also a normal part of the process to let it go, eventually. How long do you intend to punish yourself, Adam?"

"That's not what I'm doing. The accident made me realize there were things I could do so that I never had to...go through that shit again. Look, we all have issues, our history to deal with. I'm sure you have something, Skye. What was all of that stuff about not wanting to use your father's name?"

"He was a drunk. He made me miserable. I left when I was eighteen. I don't speak to him. I don't particularly trust men because of him. That's why doing this with you was such a big step for me." She stopped, blew her hair out of her eyes. "So is that enough information, or do you want to continue to divert the conversation from your own issues?"

She was strong. Smart. He liked that about her. He almost smiled.

"Look, it's not as if I never recovered. I did. That's why I had the phoenix tattooed on my back as soon as I turned eighteen. I understood even then what it represented."

"I want to see it."

He turned without another word, and Skye took in the brilliant colors, the flawless detail of a classic, Asian-style phoenix that covered his entire back. The feathered wings flowed over the muscular ripple of his shoulders; the body and the sweeping tail curved sinuously down his back to his waist. It was beautiful, the detail exquisite. The eyes of the mythical bird glowed like a pair of emeralds within the fire of the red, gold and orange plumage. She reached out to touch it, felt him shiver beneath her fingertips.

"It's magnificent. Rising out of the ashes..." She traced her finger lower, over the scar across his ribs she'd discovered earlier.

He yanked away. "Don't, Skye." His voice held a dark edge she'd never heard from him before.

"Why not? It's a part of you."

He turned back to her, his eyes blazing. "You don't get it, do you? This is a part of me I never wanted to expose to anyone. And you ripped it out of me."

"No, don't try to blame me, Adam. Some part of you wanted to tell me, had a need to, I think." Her heart was hammering in her chest. She had the sense something important was happening here, and the idea that she could lose him now scared her half to death. But she was angry, too. "I'm going home now."

He stood up, in all his naked, masculine glory. She had to look away. He was too beautiful, and it stung. "That's probably a good idea. Before we really hurt each other. I'll take you as soon as I'm dressed."

"I can call a cab."

"I said I'll take you."

Fire in his blue eyes. He was angry. But it was also about the power in him, the pure energy of who he was. She felt as though her heart was breaking. How was that possible? She'd known him less than two weeks.

She nodded, retrieved her clothes, and quietly put them on, holding back the tears that burned at her eyes, tightened her throat. Even dressed, she was shivering. With a kind of shock. With a deep dread that she may never see him again. That she shouldn't see him again.

He was dressed now, too, making him seem even more remote. "You're cold. I'll get one of my coats for you."

When he went down the hall to his bedroom, she unlocked the front door and fled into the night.

* * * *

More than a week had gone by, and Skye hadn't heard from him. Of course, he had every right to be angry with her after she'd run out on him like that. Terrible of her, she knew, but she'd had to get out of there. Curled up on her old, overstuffed velvet sofa, as she was now, she'd spent the entire week going over their conversation, dissecting it from every angle. But she always came to the same conclusion: Adam was incapable of real intimacy. He'd pretty much told her so himself, had even told her why. And he resented that she'd made him do it.

What sort of transformation would he have to go through before he could break through those old walls? If he was even willing to try.

No, he would have dumped her sooner or later, and the longer it took, the more attached she would have become, until his rejection would have been unbearable. It was nearly unbearable now.

She turned to look out the living room window at the cityscape she had always loved. But it looked bleak and lonely to her now. As empty as she felt on the inside.

She'd been drawing him all week. The table in her tiny kitchen was littered with sketches in charcoal and pencil. She'd tried to capture the musculature of his big body, the details of his strong hands, his tattoo. Mostly she'd tried to draw his face. But she couldn't seem to get the eyes right.

Finally, she'd set up her easel in the living room, close to the bay window, and painted, just a series of strokes in burnt umber and highlighted with white. The result wasn't very good. But it captured him a little better than the flatter sketches did. Still, his eyes refused to come alive for her.

She still had paint under her fingernails. She hadn't bothered to give her hands a good scrub. Hadn't bathed in a day or two. She wasn't really sure how long it had been since she'd done anything more than throw on an old pair of paint-splattered jeans and a warm thermal top, twisting her long hair up into a loose ponytail. She felt like a mess, inside and out. She couldn't get warm, no matter how high she turned up the furnace, no matter how many layers of clothing she put on. The cold came from deep inside her, like an internal stratum of ice.

So this was what a broken heart felt like. She didn't much like it. In fact, it was fucking awful.

She hadn't cried since she'd left his house. She hadn't been able to. Hadn't known anything other than this pervasive sense of pain that lay heavy in her chest every waking moment.

She dragged a pillow close and held it to her

chest, telling herself to pull herself together. She had a gallery show next month, and she was behind in her work. But she was completely devoid of inspiration.

She sighed, shook her head, and jumped at the knock at her door. Her heart leaped in her chest as she moved across the living room into the hall, and opened the door.

"Hi…um…are you Skye Ballard? I think I got your mail." A gawky young man with dark-framed glasses and a Charlie Brown sweater stood there, several envelopes in his hand.

"Oh, yes, that's me." Why did her heart drop into her stomach? Had she really expected that he would come after her? "Uh, thanks."

She took the mail, turned, and swung the door behind her. It didn't close.

She could smell him. She'd know his scent anywhere. She whirled around, her legs going weak already, and he was there. Adam. She could hardly believe it.

The mail dropped onto the wood floor, but she didn't care. What could he possibly want? And why did he have to look so damn beautiful, making her head spin?

Oh, God.

She put a hand to her hair self-consciously.

"Skye."

Even the sound of his voice made her quiver all over. She had to get a hold of herself. "Adam. What are you doing here?"

"I had to see you, talk to you."

She couldn't figure out what to say, so she

stepped aside and let him in. Her pulse was racing with fear, with a yearning so strong she could hardly stand it. She led him into the living room, gestured for him to sit down, but he went immediately to the painting by the window.

"It's me."

She bit her lip. "Yes."

"You're very good."

"It's awful. It's not...I can't get it right."

When he turned, his gaze was full of emotion. Shocking, to see his face like that. "No, Skye. You had it right all along."

"What do you mean?"

Two long strides and he was right in front of her. He took her shoulders in his hands, held on tight. Her heart hammered as though it would pound right out of her chest. And she was going weak all over from his touch, his scent, from the nearness of him.

"Damn it, Skye, all the way over here, I knew exactly what I needed to say to you. But now I'm here, and...you're so fucking beautiful, I'm speechless. And that's never happened to me before."

Tears stung her eyes, but she had to laugh. "I look like hell."

He shook his head, his blue eyes dark, intense. "You look perfect. That's why I'm here. You are perfect, and I'm an idiot to pass that up. You are perfect for me."

"I don't understand."

"That last night...everything you said was true. I knew it. I was just too damn stubborn to listen.

And what did that get me? A fucking miserable week without you."

"It's been eight days," she said quietly.

He nodded. "Eight long days with me driving myself crazy thinking about you, needing you. I know I'm an asshole, Skye. I'm sorry, I truly am sorry. And I know we hardly know each other. But we *do*. Do you know what I mean?"

"Yes. I know exactly."

She was beginning to warm up, finally. The heat started where his hands were planted on her shoulders, spread down into her belly. It was the intensity of the physical chemistry between them; there was no denying it. But it was something more, too. She could see it on his face. Felt it in every beat of her heart.

"Tell me what this means, Adam. Please."

"I don't know. This is all new to me. But I want to find out."

He stroked her cheeks with his thumbs, bent down and kissed her. His lips were the sweetest thing she'd ever tasted. And his hands holding her face felt safe and warm.

He moved her to the sofa, laid her down, lowered his body over hers. He was still kissing her, his tongue doing lovely things to her mouth, sending heat lancing through her body. Her breasts filled, ached, and when he crushed her body to his, she wanted nothing more than to be right there, with him.

"Touch me, Adam. Be with me."

"That's all I want, Skye," he murmured, taking her clothes off, raining kisses over her shoulders, her breasts, her belly.

This was new to her, too, allowing herself to feel this way about a man, wanting him to feel the same way about her. Even though neither of them knew exactly where they were going, they would explore the possibilities together.

In moments, they were both naked, and he was poised over her body. She wrapped her arms around his neck and opened to him. Completely. And when he entered her, she was lost in his embrace. For the first time in her life, she allowed herself to be.

Adam had been right, in their very first conversation. She'd had to break control, to let it go. Finally, she'd found the way. With him.

Submissive Secrets
Eliza Gayle

Also by Eliza Gayle

Taken By Tarot

"Dragon's Fate" from
Phaze Fantasies, Vol. III

Pentacles of Magick: The Bonding

Pentacles of Magick: The Burning

Chapter One

The familiar rush of cool air enveloped Carli as she opened her front door and walked inside. The warming scent of fresh baked apples and the soft glow of her dimmed kitchen lights welcomed her as usual. Kicking off her boots and hanging her jacket on a hook, she could think of little else besides a cold beer and a long soak in her Jacuzzi tub. Rolling her shoulders, she winced as the muscles tightened painfully.

What I need is a man, someone to help release some of this tension.

The day had not gone well. When she proved her latest client's husband to be a lying, cheating bastard, as usual, the woman had not been grateful for the news and became hysterical. Carli had spent the last hour being yelled at and slapped in the face, and then, to add insult to injury, she had to mop up buckets of tears. *I can't believe she caught me off guard on that one.* She reached up and touched her still-throbbing cheek. Sometimes it sucked being a private investigator.

When had her life taken such a dark turn? She felt a far cry from her days as a sniper in the Marine Corps. Her time in the military had been exciting, a real thrill a minute. Traveling all over the world, she led a group of hunky soldiers who jumped at her every command. Carli even got to play with big guns. She especially loved the big guns. Her life had been perfect. Except one thing...Aidan.

She tried everything to forget him. Work. Exercise. Sex—lots of sex. But nothing could erase the memories of her sweet Aidan. Her nipples tightened, as always, when thoughts of him and his long lanky frame pressed tightly against hers came to mind. While not overly muscled, his youthful body had been firm and fit. Shaking her head, she did her best to push back the memories before she ended up with either a headache or a bleeding heart once again. Eight years had passed since she'd seen him last. Walking away from him was her biggest mistake. When would she be able to forget?

"Uh..."

She froze in mid step.

What the hell was that? Someone's in my house. Dammit. I do not fucking need this right now.

Automatically she reached behind her and pulled her Glock from the waistband of her tight jeans. Slipping the safety off, she crept down the hallway in the direction of the sound. A visual sweep of the kitchen revealed nothing. Moving toward her bedroom, she detected someone's light breathing.

Gun at the ready, she eased into her room, looking for her intruder. The gentle snoring became louder, and as she glanced to the bed in the corner she caught sight of a glorious full moon shining up.

Holy shit! There's a naked man sleeping in my bed, with the finest ass I have ever seen.

As she stepped closer to the bed, even more of

his naked body came into view. The deeply tanned skin and corded muscle indicated he spent a great deal of time working outside. His jet black hair fanning across her pillow appeared a little too long. The soft light spilling from the bathroom bathed his body with just enough illumination for her to see plenty. That amazing ass connected to huge muscular thighs, and for a split second, she thought about what it would be like to have those hard muscles pressed against her body.

Get a grip. He's a complete stranger. An intruder in your home and you're fantasizing about his legs?

Gripping her gun tighter, she opened her mouth to demand what the hell he was doing in her bed, when he gently rolled over on to his back. With the first glance of his chest, liquid pooled in her panties. His gloriously sculpted pecs with a sprinkling of hair narrowed down to a trail leading to…

Stop! Quit thinking with your pussy and use your brain.

She shook her head to clear the fog threatening to take over and looked up to his face to see if she could identify him.

Time stopped. She couldn't breathe. Her chest constricted. Her arm holding the gun went slack.

She hissed, a quick intake of breath.

The shock of seeing him in her bed after all this time rattled through her brain, and before she could process what was happening, a strong hand circled her wrist, pulling her toward the bed. With no time to react she quickly found herself pinned underneath him, staring into his steel blue eyes.

"Jesus Christ, Carli, you could have gotten one of

us killed, sneaking up on me like that."

Her airway constricted as she tried to form words. "Aidan," she croaked out. Realizing he'd put too much pressure on her lungs, he shifted to the side, placing more of his weight on his arm.

"What the hell are you doing in my bed?" Not that she was complaining, as this was what she'd been dreaming about for so many years. Still, for him to show up after all these years, break into her house and then crawl into her bed seemed a little over the top. "I could have shot *you*."

"What's wrong, baby? You're not happy to see me?" The rich timbre of his voice resonated deep in her body, sparking a reaction she wasn't quite ready for. Yet, the sarcastic overtones caused the hair on her neck to bristle, giving her a bad feeling. She learned long ago to listen to those instincts. They hadn't failed her yet, and she didn't think they would now.

"You've got some nerve showing up after all this time and making yourself comfortable like this." She placed her hands on his chest to give him a quick shove. "In my house."

First mistake.

The velvety soft skin over hard muscle and bone made her fingers itch with the need to stroke his chest and maybe more. Placing her palms flat on his chiseled chest again, she shoved. Hard. Nothing happened. His body didn't move an inch.

"Get off of me. You're crushing me. Dammit. I want you to tell me what the hell is going on here." She squirmed against him, trying to shake him loose.

Second mistake.

His cock hardened and lengthened against the inside of her thigh. The more she struggled, the more it grew. Despite her annoyance with him, her pulse quickened, and her clit throbbed.

"Not yet, baby. I'm liking this position a whole lot right now." He grabbed her hands from his chest and raised them above her head, pinning her to the mattress.

Before she could even pant a token protest, he crushed her mouth with a hard, demanding kiss. His tongue pushed between her taut lips, forcing her to allow him entry. His tongue tangled with hers in a fierce sensual battle. For a moment more, she considered fighting him, but it was too good. It had been too long. She needed this. Needed him.

His forcefulness was unexpected but welcomed. She needed...no, desired a man who took what he wanted in bed. She liked her sex a little on the rough side anyway. Although she would have never expected this from Aidan, the pressure and intensity of his kiss quickly pushed her past her ability to reason this situation out. Her hips bucked against his hard cock, digging into her thigh. She struggled to free her arms. She had to touch him. He simply tightened his hold. She wouldn't get loose until he let her.

Instead of releasing her, he nestled his cock right into the vee of her thighs, pressing right against her clit. She couldn't hold back the moan that escaped. This unexpected show of dominance fed her need. A few more thrusts of his cock, and she experienced her first fully clothed orgasm.

Chapter Two

He'd known finding him naked in her bed would likely unnerve Carli, but he didn't expect this much reaction.

God, she felt good.

He didn't want to stop. He wanted to tear her clothes from her athletic body and force his throbbing dick up her juicy pussy. Releasing Carli's mouth, he trailed his lips along her jaw and neck, nipping at her sensitive skin as he went. When he reached her breasts, he rubbed his cheek against the cool silk of her shirt, feeling her distended nipple. Carli arched her back into his touch, begging for more.

Maintaining his grip on her wrists with one hand, Aidan reached underneath her shirt pulling the fabric out of his way, exposing her bright rosy nipple. Instead of laving her gently with his tongue as she anticipated, he bit her nipple with a quick sharp bite. She didn't protest his roughness but instead surged against him, pleading for more.

Unfortunately, looking back up at her face, flushed with her arousal, brought Aidan's memories crashing back down. He remembered the last time he'd seen her, and the pain of his heart splitting in two when she told him, just before their wedding, that she needed something more. Needed to travel. Needed to get away from him for a while. In the end, the anger caused by her betrayal had won out and he'd opted to leave town.

Rifling through her personal belongings when he entered her home had brought out a need in him he thought long buried. As much as he wanted to fuck her mindless, he couldn't do this. Couldn't screw Carli now without thinking of the girl back then. The girl who crushed his heart, leaving him behind as she went to explore the world. As his lust subsided, cold anger took its place. He released her arms and stood. He had a job to do, and reliving old times with Carli would only fuck that up.

He turned his back on her as he reached to the floor for his discarded jeans. Quickly pulling them up, not even bothering to button them before turning back around to face her. The expression on her face remained blank, but her eyes sparked with repressed emotion.

"I can't do this, Carli." His gut tightened at the pain he saw flicker across her face.

She looked up at the ceiling and tunneled her fingers through her long chestnut locks, probably trying to get control of her body just as he did.

With a pronounced sigh, she nailed him with a steely stare. "Why are you here, Aidan? What brings you back to my bed after all these years?" she bit out, her voice laced with cold sarcasm.

Boldly lying back against the pillows, she crossed her arms behind her head, further baring her breast to him, and waited for his answer.

"I'm here on assignment. I need your

cooperation." He paused, waiting for a reaction that never materialized.

Oh, she's good. Very good at keeping her cool when it counted.

Aidan knew Carli had tried several times over the last couple of years to find him, as his organization kept tabs on that kind of information. But he didn't want to be found. If not for this mission, he would never have returned to this old town. Aidan didn't need the physical reminder of where he came from or the circumstances under which he had left. The sooner Aidan got the information he needed from Carli, the sooner he would be out of here. In the meantime, he had no intention of letting her get to him. No one got to him anymore. Her leaving him taught him how to build barriers to shield his heart. At least he could thank her for that.

* * * *

Carli waited. Waited for Aidan to reveal the real reason for being in *her* house. Over the years she had perfected the art of patience. It was what made her so good at what she did—both as a sniper and now as an investigator. To further throw Aidan off, she struck a more casual, carefree pose by tucking her hands behind her neck and crossing her ankles. She could wait him out.

Looking over at him standing in front of her dresser, she couldn't help marvel at the changes in his appearance. Gone was the tall, lanky nineteen-year-old who stole her heart. Replaced with this tall, powerful, very muscled, devilishly handsome man. She wondered what else about him had changed.

"I need your help locating someone." His long pause led her to believe he was definitely avoiding telling her more. What could he be up to that would be hard for her to handle? His reluctance was a clear sign that he didn't trust her.

Then why come to me? Why not get someone else, anyone else to help him?

"Why me? If you don't really want to be here with me, why not find someone else to help you?" Sensing she wasn't going to like his answers, she braced herself for the other shoe to drop.

"It's—It's your brother, Carli. I'm here to gather some information that will help me find him. He is wanted for treason against the U.S. government."

Thunk.

The shoe dropped.

* * * *

"What? Are you crazy?" Sitting up, her body tensed. Anger flushed her face, and she expected him to back away. He didn't. "My brother has been serving as an intelligence officer in the U.S. Navy for over six years. How dare you make such crazy accusations?" She stepped forward, getting right in his face. "You better explain yourself right now."

He smirked. He couldn't help himself. Her eyes sparking with anger were even more arousing than before. He relished the thought that she might tackle him and kick his ass. Aidan would love to take the time to get down and dirty with her and teach her a lesson or two. Lessons she would never forget. He hadn't. He still harbored a lot of resentment toward her and would love to take the time to have it out with her.

But he had a job to do, and do it he would. He couldn't afford to get wrapped up in the past, even if it came in a tight body that screamed *fuck me* with every move.

"A couple of days ago, we intercepted a message between your brother, Cliff, and a top terrorist leader. Twelve hours later, Cliff disappeared." He didn't try to soften the blow he knew this news would create. Aidan needed to see and analyze every reaction Carli had to assure himself she wasn't somehow involved. "We know how close you and your twin are, so we expect either you already know where he is or he will be contacting you soon to let you know something."

His gut told him that no way would Carli be involved in anything like this. Hell, he was even surprised her brother Cliff would be. Her face paled from the shock of his words, confirming his instincts. She knew absolutely nothing of this. Cliff had somehow managed to not only get himself involved in an international incident, but keep the news from his twin sister. *Interesting.*

She staggered back, and he snaked his arm around her waist to steady her. Taking some deep breaths to calm herself, Carli managed a whisper. "This is a mistake. Cliff would never do anything like this. He must be in some sort of trouble. I have to help him."

* * * *

She grabbed his shoulders, trying to shake him. Make him see the truth in her eyes. After all they had been through, how could he suspect her own flesh and blood of treason?

"Wait a damn minute!" She backed away from him. "Why are you really here? Do you think I have something to do with this? Am I a suspect?"

He hesitated.

So that's how it was. She was under investigation along with her brother. Blinded by anger, she scooped up her gun from the floor and aimed it dead center at his chest.

"Whoa, Carli." He threw his hands out in surrender. "There's no need for that. I don't personally suspect that you are involved in anything. I'm just here to gather information and wait to see if your brother contacts you."

"Why should I believe you?" Tears were welling in Carli's eyes, but she would be damned if she allowed them to fall. All these years, she waited for him to return so she could beg his forgiveness, and instead he showed up here with a charge of treason, ready to arrest her brother and possibly her, too.

"Believe me? Why wouldn't you?" he frowned. "Have I ever lied to you?" No, he hadn't lied. Just disappeared and left her frustrated and confused for far too long. Too much had happened, and too much time had passed. She couldn't tell him now that she had come back six weeks later, prepared to beg his forgiveness for leaving him, only to find him gone without a trace. The only man she'd ever loved was standing in front of her. He wasn't nineteen anymore, and it was clear he didn't have feelings for her.

She lowered the gun. "I don't trust you, Aidan."

"Not a problem, sweetheart. You don't have to trust me. Just cooperate with me. The sooner you do, the sooner I'll be back on my way to Washington and back out of your life, just like you want."

A flash of wild grief ripped through her, gripping her in panic and fear, at the thought of him leaving her again. Despite everything, she craved another chance.

* * * *

Aidan finished dressing and joined Carli in the living room. She had changed into a tank top and running shorts and now lounged on the couch with her eyes closed. He took this time to appreciate her long tanned legs. Despite what happened between them in the past, he wanted those legs wrapped around his waist as he plunged his cock into her tight, wet pussy. His already half-hard dick stiffened at the images that produced.

Spending time with Carli would be harder than he'd originally thought if he didn't get his sexual urges for her under control.

Carli shifted slightly on the couch, exposing a small bare patch of silky skin on her belly that beckoned to him. Moving to the couch, he loomed over her, considering his options.

"Stop staring at me as if you want to bite me." She'd opened her eyes while he'd been staring at her naked skin. He did want to bite her. Maybe even spank her. Definitely fuck her. She stirred some longing deep inside him that he refused to think about it. He couldn't. No, wouldn't give her or any other woman the chance to hurt him again. If he took her now, it would just be sex. He was in control.

His gaze dropped from her eyes to her shoulders and traveled down to her breasts. Her nipples peaked under the thin cloth, and unable to resist, he reached down and pinched one between his thumb and forefinger. A quiet moan escaped Carli's lips, quickening her breath. Aidan couldn't ignore the blatant invitation in her eyes as his control faltered, and he reached down, ripping the tank top from her body.

Carli gasped. Her womb clenched, and her pulse pounded. Pure male lust adorned his face as he stared at her exposed breasts. She knew he wanted her, but something was holding him back. Determined to completely break his control, she fondled her own nipples, rolling them tightly between her fingers. The sensations rippled along her skin, leaving her panting. Performing for him turned her on, and he clearly liked it, as evidenced by the fabric of his jeans pressing tightly across his engorged sex.

"Take your shorts off. Now." The husky sound of his demand stoked her need.

Her pussy flooded with moisture as she grabbed the waistband of her running shorts and rolled them down her legs, leaving her completely naked. He remained fully clothed. The air against her bare cunt did nothing to cool her body. She was more enflamed than ever. She inched her thighs apart, wondering if he liked a shaved pussy.

Now she ached to see him naked. To memorize the changes in his body. "I want to see you."

He stood so close that the heat radiating from his body scorched her.

"Not yet. Not until I say so."

A quiver surged through her veins, realizing he planned to make her beg. Already her clit throbbed for his touch. It wouldn't be long, and she would beg him to make her come. Scooping her up from the couch, Aidan carried her back to the bedroom, putting her down next to the bed. He could have just as easily laid her on the bed, but she suspected he had a different plan for her. A test of sorts.

"Get on the bed," he ordered her.

Despite her penchant for dominance, her first instinct was to tell him to go to hell, but his rough demanding voice gave her chills at the thought of what could be coming.

He reached for the nightstand, and panic rose up in the back of her throat. "Wait!" she screamed at him, afraid of what he would think or say if he knew everything she kept in her drawers.

"It's too late, baby, I've already seen what you keep in there. I know what you really want. I'm more than man enough to handle it and then some."

"What do you mean you already know? You snooped through my house when I wasn't here?" Anger coursed through her veins, feeding her arousal. She was furious with him, but at the same time, if he didn't fuck her soon, she was going to go insane.

He threw her a look that he knew told herhe was done talking. Now she would just have to wait and see what he did next.

"Lie back down on the bed, and spread your legs for me." She hesitated, unsure of how far she wanted to take this with him. "If you don't do it, I will tie you down." He growled at her, indicating that he hung onto his control by a thread.

Carli slowly crawled up the bed, wiggling her ass at him before rolling onto her back and spreading her legs wide. But instead of waiting to see what he would do, she slid her hand down to her pussy and ran her fingers along the slit, coating herself with her juices. When she pinched her swollen clit with her fingers, her body jerked in reaction. Slipping two fingers inside, she began pumping them slowly in and out, setting her body aflame with need.

"Oh, God, Carli. That has got to be the hottest thing I've ever seen." His voice was a hoarse whisper. Aidan quickly undressed and settled himself between her thighs, watching her pleasure herself. "Tilt your hand to the side just a bit, baby."

She followed his orders, thighs quivering in anticipation. He brought his mouth down to her pussy and flicked her clit with his tongue.

That was all it took for her control to completely shatter, and she begged. "Aidan, please, you've got to fuck me. Hard. Right now."

Before he could answer, the exquisite torture his tongue performed became too much, and her body exploded. Her muscles clamped down on her own fingers as the release continued under the onslaught of his tongue.

Bringing his cock to her opening, he moved her hand and parted her sensitive folds with his fingers. In one swift move, he slammed his shaft all the way to the hilt, tormenting her quaking flesh. Without hesitation, he continued thrusting his cock into her cunt as she screamed her pleasure, begging for more. Grabbing her nipples, Carli squeezed hard, adding the pleasure-pain sensation she loved to his cock, slamming into her sweat-soaked body.

Aidan moaned and roared as his semen spurted inside her womb. Frantically pumping her pussy against his cock, with one last deep thrust, her second orgasm burst free.

Finally, he had come home.

Despite all the years of pain and suffering, she knew she loved him with her heart and soul, and didn't think she could let him go...again. As their bodies trembled together, she worried whether she could find a way to make him stay.

Chapter Three

Damn, Carli had the hottest cunt on the planet. It had only been an hour since she had given him the best goddamn orgasm of his life, but as she stirred next to him, rubbing her soft ass against his dick, he wanted her again.

She mumbled something he couldn't understand as she continued rubbing against him. Slipping his hand between her thighs, he found her pussy slick and hot. Grasping his hard cock and settling it at her slit, he slid home, deep into her tight sex. Carli jerked in surprise at the initial invasion but then relaxed, allowing him to set the pace. This time he took her slow and easy, loving the sounds of her pussy trying to suck him back in every time he withdrew. Her muscles gripped him like a vise.

Her soft moans turned to loud pleas as she neared her release. He couldn't resist running his fingers through the crack of her lush ass, tenderly probing the tight rosebud of her backside. He wouldn't be able to hold back much longer but wanted to feel her muscles clamping down on his cock as they both came. Aidan's fingers slid forward and lightly pinched her clit, sending her over the edge where he quickly followed.

As his softening cock slipped from her sex, she

turned and faced him. Her eyes glowed with an emotion, and he couldn't dare speak as she pressed her full lips to his.

"You are an amazing lover. I can't believe how much I have missed it." He stiffened at her words. Her referring to their past was like dousing him with a bucket of ice water. He quickly reminded himself that he was here to perform a job, and this was just sex between two consenting adults.

Albeit mind-blowing, toe-curling, amazing sex.

He couldn't afford to let emotions for her sneak up on him. Instead of responding to her compliment, he quickly changed the subject to less intimate issues.

"Carli, when was the last time you spoke with your brother?" Watching her face for any telltale signs of lying, he found nothing. Her eyes went from gazing at him in sweet adoration to a carefully blanked mask in a matter of seconds.

"Last Sunday. We talk every week on Sunday night," she managed through clenched teeth. She rose from the bed and stomped over to the dresser grabbing some items from the top. "You just want to talk about Cliff? Fine. But not until I get cleaned up. I've had a long, trying day, and the least I deserve before my interrogation is a shower."

He started to tell her he wasn't interrogating her, but she slammed the bathroom door before he had a chance.

Well, that's one way to get us back on track.

He hurriedly dressed himself and headed for the kitchen. Images of her rubbing soap over her naked breasts and flat belly nearly drove him to the bathroom to fuck her all over again. He wondered again if the next few days were going to be enough to get her out of his system once and for all.

* * * *

Carli walked in the kitchen to find Aidan cooking at the stove. She leaned against the doorjamb and watched, her body relaxed, non-threatening. Without even realizing it, he had set the perfect domestic scene. A man cooking for his woman…

Only this wasn't their home, and he wasn't taking care of her, he was questioning her.

He had dressed in his jeans and left his feet bare. His broad shoulders tapered down to a lean, narrow waist, where his jeans cupped his gorgeous butt. Having her hands on his body again had been like a totally new experience. She remembered him from their youth, but their changes brought a whole new level of heat to their sex together. It would be wonderful if they could just pick up where they left off before she ruined everything. But eight years was a long time.

People change.

Feelings change.

Right now she had as many questions for him as he probably had for her. Starting with where the hell had he been for these last eight years?

She'd searched for him for two years before giving up. Although not completely. Every year on the anniversary of her dumb-ass mistake, she spent a day or two searching again. Nothing. It was as if he had dropped off the face of the earth.

Now here he was in her kitchen. Every wish fulfilled. Except he wasn't here for her. He was looking for Cliff and apparently prepared to use any method available to get what he wanted from her.

He turned slowly from the stove, catching her examination. Their gazes locked, and his tight expression relaxed into a smile. Try as she might, she couldn't hold out against that. Releasing an audible breath, she allowed the tension to ease from her body as she slid into the chair across from him.

"This looks great. I'm starving." She dug in, scooping a large forkful into her mouth. As she savored the spicy sausage dish, a low moan escaped her lips.

"Babe, I'll take that as your approval of my cooking," he teased. "But keep moaning like that, and I'm likely to have *you* for dinner." The smile in his eyes promised erotic fun as images of what they had just done flashed through her mind. Her nipples tightened in anticipation, and she was sorely tempted. Shoving those thoughts aside, she knew it was time to face the elephant in the room. She needed answers and needed them now.

"Nice try, Aidan. But it's not going to work. Before I cooperate with you any further, you have to answer a few of my questions." She watched his expression change to serious and wished there were another way.

"Fine. I'll answer as much as I can without compromising myself. Carli, you have to know that a lot of what I do is on a need-to-know basis." She took a deep breath, thinking back to all the times she'd come up empty in her search for him.

Why would he disappear like that?

"Who do you work for?" When he didn't answer, she wondered why. It was a simple question, requiring a simple answer.

He shifted in his seat, resting his arms behind his head. "I work for a private government organization. Before you ask which one," shifting again, "I'm not at liberty to divulge that information."

She slammed her hands down on the kitchen table. "Is this how it's going to be? I'll ask a question, any question, and you'll tell me you can't say? How about this? What exactly has my brother done, and what evidence is there against him?

"There is some important intel your brother recently found that is now missing from his office along with him."

She waited for him to say more, but instead he sat there with a tight-lipped, closed expression.

"What kind of intel?"

"You know I can't tell you that. All I can say is that it is of utmost urgency to national security."

"This is bullshit and you know it." She rose in one fluid motion, taking deep, calming breaths to recapture her composure. As casually as she could manage, she asked, "Where have you been these past eight years?" To her dismay, her voice broke.

His eyebrows shot up in surprise. Clearly that wasn't the question he had been expecting.

"What? Why? What difference does it make?"

"It makes a difference to me, that's why." She heard her voice and cringed. She sounded so desperate.

"Why would my whereabouts make a difference to you after all this time?" His question was stilted and bitter.

She backed away from the table, her jaw

tightening. She had gone too far. She couldn't bear the thought of him knowing she had been pining for him all these years. Sure, she dated other men, but as long as she had hopes of finding Aidan one day, none of those men could get past the first date.

Hell, if she hadn't been so desperate for hard sex now and again, she probably wouldn't have dated at all. Could she help it if being dominated sexually by a man was such a thrill? It was the one thing about herself that she'd always been afraid to tell Aidan. She'd been too young to face her dark desires openly and instead ran away from his love in search of something more, hoping it would fill the need. It didn't.

Aidan grasped Carli's elbow and pushed her against the wall. His breath caressed her ear. "What aren't you telling me?" The full length of his body crushed against her backside; his erection pressed between the cheeks of her ass. The heat of his cock burned straight through the thin material of her shorts. Her senses were overloaded, and she couldn't find the words to answer.

"Damn it, Carli, tell me. If you don't tell me what you're hiding, I will spank it out of you."

Her pussy flooded with her cream at his words. She hated to admit, even to herself, how much his aggressiveness aroused her. She tried to get a grip before she lost complete control.

"I was just curious is all," she lied.

His muscles flexed in his biceps as he gripped her tighter. She struggled against him, trying to break loose.

"Are you lying to me? 'Cause I think you are."

His lips nuzzled her neck gently; then without warning, he bit her. Not a little nip, but a bite that would leave a mark. The pleasure-pain sensation coursed through her heated blood as she wiggled her bottom against his hard erection.

"You like that, don't you?"

"No," she pushed out through heavy pants.

"Well, then, I guess you'll really hate this." Releasing one of her arms, he pushed her tighter against the wall with his body to hold her firmly in place.

Grasping the waistband of her thin shorts, he yanked them down around her knees. Plunging two fingers into the passion-swollen folds of her slick cunt, he pulled a cry from her trembling body.

"Tell me, now!" He pumped his fingers, edging her closer to her release. She thrust her hips, riding his fingers hard on the brink of her orgasm. Slowing his pace, Aidan slid a third finger into her pussy, coating it with her juices. Easing the third finger along the seam between her pussy and her ass, he roughly pressed the lubricated finger against the tighter opening.

She whimpered. She pushed her bottom against his hand, begging for penetration, but Aidan held back, waiting for her answer.

"Carli, baby, tell me what I want to know, or I stop right now."

"Please—don't—stop," she gasped. "I'll tell you."

In response, he pushed his finger in, just to the first knuckle. And waited. Her body was on fire, and she couldn't let him stop now. She wiggled and thrashed, trying to get him to move his fingers, to satisfy her aching body. He held strong and firm, barely allowing her to move.

"I've been searching for you every year since you left."

He stilled again.

The waiting was killing her. She was too close to the edge. "Please, Aidan, fuck me."

"Why, baby? Why have you been searching for me?" He eased his finger in a little more. She bucked, needing more.

"Because I still love you!" she bellowed, as he slid his finger all the way to the hilt, scraping against tender flesh, causing her body to explode, pussy and ass gripping his fingers.

Chapter Four

Aidan sucked in a breath, his heart hammering in his chest. He felt restless and irritable. His cock burned with a fever to plunge into her body. He needed her so badly. But she had lied to him. Even in the midst of a punishing orgasm, she cunningly told him what she thought he wanted to hear.

Too bad she was wrong.

He had accepted long ago she didn't love him. They were young and had a great time together, but she had been grasping for more. More of what, he hadn't understood then, but he was starting to get an idea from the way she responded to his urges to control her. Not to mention the toys and books he'd found in her bedroom.

Easing his fingers from her sated body, he gently released his hold on her and stepped back. She looked briefly over her shoulder before quickly pulling herself together. Not knowing what to say, he shook his head and walked back to his seat at the table.

Could it be? Was the answer right there in front of him every time he fucked her?

Or was this all about her brother?

He began analyzing what her possible motives

could be, at least as much as his throbbing cock would allow. Was he wrong about her and her brother? Could she know more than she let on? His gut still told him he wasn't wrong, but he also wasn't a fool, so he would take it into consideration and keep a closer eye on her actions and reactions. She probably either knew where her brother was or at least a very good idea of where he could be. He would have to work on that.

But first he needed to figure out why she was looking at him with such a horrified expression, eyes wide in shock. She had barely moved since he sat down. She just kept glaring at him as if he had done something wrong. He exhaled a sigh of relief when she collected herself and sat back down.

"Do you still want to know where I have been these past eight years?" Reaching across the table, he clasped her hand in his, absently rubbing his thumb back and forth across her palm.

Her closed expression softened just a bit as she nodded her head.

"One week after you left for the Corps, I traded in my truck for a bike and took off for the open road." The memories flooded his mind as he thought back to his ignorant self back then. "As much as I had planned to settle in this town forever, as soon as you left, I couldn't wait to get away."

Actually the pain of her leaving him had torn him in two, and he couldn't bear to be in their town without her. He couldn't tell her that. Wouldn't bare that much of his pain to her again.

"After a few months, I hooked up with a gang of bikers, started getting into trouble."

The things he had seen and done had changed him forever. The drugs, the violence, and God—the women. He'd done his best to erase her from his mind by fucking a different woman every day.

"I'm lucky I didn't end up dead or in jail."

She did her best to avoid eye contact, but he saw the moisture pooling in her eyes as he told her what he'd done.

"About a year later, we holed up in this great little town down in Texas, and something there clicked with me, and I decided to stay. After two years of intense physical and investigations training with a local P.I., a client propositioned me about working for an elite government agency."

"Black Ops," she whispered. He didn't respond. Couldn't. He had already told her too much. "That's why I could never find a record of you anywhere in the U.S. Your records have all been erased as if you never existed."

"That's all there is to my story. Now it's your turn. Are you going to cooperate with me?"

She pulled her hand from his grasp and sat back in her chair, closing her eyes as if contemplating what to do. Her chestnut-colored hair was a riot of curls framing her oval face. He wanted to lick the freckles that were sprinkled across her face. Her skin was scented of musk, but he knew it tasted like honey.

He couldn't stop thinking about burying himself deep in her channel. He was drawn to her. Couldn't get enough of her. Damn, what was he going to do about her? He had to get her out of his system.

"Aidan, it may have been eight years since

you've been around Cliff, but he's my twin, and you know him as well as you know me. Do you really think he is guilty?"

"It doesn't matter what I think. That's not my job. I'm just trying to locate him, not judge him."

"It matters to me."

"Carli, eight years ago, I probably would have sworn I knew the two of you so well you could never be guilty of any crime. But when you left me, you shocked me to the core. So obviously, I didn't know you as well as I thought."

"I really don't know where he is at the moment. I never even sensed he was in any kind of trouble when I spoke to him last week. I tried calling his cell phone after I showered but just got his voicemail. I'm really worried about him, since he didn't even try to contact me." She crossed her arms across her chest, closing him out. "That's just not like him. We don't keep secrets from each other."

"It's damn suspicious, Carli."

"What will you do now?"

"I have to stay here until he is found. You have been placed in my protective custody until he shows up."

"You don't trust me either, do you?" she quietly asked. The pain visible in her eyes caught him off guard. Without his consent, something shifted deep inside. He began to crack.

"It's no longer a matter of trust. It's just a job." He wanted to reach over and comfort her, but she shut down.

"I've had all I can take for one day. I'm going to bed. You're welcome to the guest bedroom." She turned to leave.

"Carli, why have you *really* continued to look for me after all these years? Is there something more I don't know?"

Her shoulders sagged in resignation. "A few short weeks after I joined the Corps, I realized what a mistake I had made with you, and I came back to find you, but you were gone. I've searched for you ever since."

"Wait, that's not enough. Why did you really run away? If you still love me as you say, then tell me what drove you to run?"

She didn't turn back or say anything else. She just walked down the hall to her room and closed herself inside, leaving him to ponder his own unanswered questions.

Chapter Five

Stalking across her bedroom floor, she viciously ran her fingers through her messy hair. How could he be so damn calm and cool after what we just did? Remembering the delicious force he had used on her, her nipples peaked and her pussy heated. She needed to get his focus off her brother and back on to their relationship, but he was making it damned difficult.

She scooped her cell phone off the nightstand and put in another call to her brother. The phone rang once and then, "Hi, this is Cliff, leave me a message and I'll get back to you."

Straight to voicemail. *He doesn't even have the damn thing turned on.* She tossed the phone onto the bed and stomped across the room. She was certain whatever he was mixed up in, they would be able to clear it up. No way would he turn criminal. Now, if she could just get Aidan to listen to her. Not just about Cliff, but about them. *Maybe after I get some sleep, I can deal with Aidan's attitude and my brother.*

Discarding all of her clothes, Carli slipped under the covers and curled onto her side. She tossed and turned. She flipped and flopped and then tossed some more. Looking at the red glowing digital readout of her bedside clock, Carli realized she had been lying there restless and awake for almost two hours.

"Fuck this. Since when do I lay around trying to figure out what to do? I know what I want, and I am going to get it, whether he likes it or not."

With a self-satisfied smile she walked toward her door buck naked. She was going to get her man once and for all. She wasted eight years searching and waiting for her chance to make amends, and now she couldn't wait one more second.

Before she could get out of her room, her phone beeped three times in quick succession, signaling a text message had just come through. She anxiously grabbed the phone, hitting the SMS button to retrieve the message.

Carli, my latest mission went a little off track. Due to some extremely sensitive intel I intercepted, it was necessary to remove myself to a safer location until the time is right for disclosure. Knowing Aidan is with you is a huge relief and will make this situation easier to resolve. Trust me when I say everything will be fine in just a few days. I can't tell you anymore but I know you understand. I'll call you as soon as I can. Don't do anything rash and trust Aidan to keep you safe. Love, Cliff

"A little off track? There is nothing little about this situation." Relieved to know that her brother was okay, Carli decided to show the message to Aidan.

* * * *

Slipping quietly into the spare bedroom, she stood just inside the door, waiting for her eyes to adjust to the darkness. When she could see, she glanced over at the bed to find it empty.

Huh. Must have decided to sleep on the couch.

She turned and headed for the living room.

Standing at the foot of the empty couch, she wondered where he went. He'd been adamant about not leaving her alone, so she suspected he hadn't gone far.

She headed for the balcony to get a quick look around the outside property. At three a.m., there shouldn't have been any activity out there. She expected to see him strolling the grounds. Padding quietly over to the railing, she peered over the lawn. She turned with a start when someone touched her arm.

"Holy shit, give me a heart attack, why don't you?"

He stood transfixed, studying her intently. His gaze left her eyes and traveled along her shoulders and down to her breasts. Her nipples hardened to tight points under his scrutiny. Her breath quickened. A few moments later, his eyes traveled down her flat, tanned belly to her bare mound, which had already moistened under his perusal.

"An exhibitionist now, I see." His hands trembled slightly as he brushed her wild curls from her cheek.

"I expected to find you asleep, not out here hiding on the balcony," she answered over her racing pulse. Her words were hurried.

"Couldn't sleep. Hard to let go when you drop a bomb like that on me." His husky voice betrayed some of his feelings, despite the regret in his eyes.

She held up the cell phone so he noticed it, rather than her body. "I came to show you this."

"What is it?" He took the offered phone from her

hand, expecting her to say she got a call from her brother.

"Cliff just sent me a text message, and I thought you would want to see it." She pressed the button, and a message time-stamped just minutes ago scrolled across the screen.

His features turned grim as he read the message illuminated on the cell. It might not have given him the information he needed to complete his mission, but it did give her a measure of relief. Her brother was in control of the situation, just as she had expected, and more than likely, in a few days, he would show up at her doorstep as if nothing ever happened.

"Is this it?" He held out the phone to her, questioning. "Is this the only reason you came out here to see me? Because this could have waited until morning and doesn't really explain why you're standing there nude." He came close, looking down at her for an answer.

Biting her lip, she looked away.

"Carli, why did you leave me, baby? I know there's more to it than you just weren't ready to settle down until you saw the world. We could have traveled together." A small hitch in his voice surprised her.

She shook her head in denial; even now she feared his rejection. He stilled her movements by gently taking her head in his hands, brushing his lips against her mouth. He kissed her surprisingly gently, considering how frustrated she knew him to be. His tenderness sparked the flame low in her belly, and she was quickly engulfed with desire. Hungrily, she kissed him back, covering his mouth with hers. Forcing her tongue inside his mouth, she devoured him in one swift move.

Wrenching his mouth free, he released her. "Carli, I have to know. Being here with you again has brought forward all the memories of what your leaving did to me. If you have any hope of us moving past this, you have to tell me the truth. Nothing short will do." His magnetic and compelling eyes burned into hers, demanding the truth from her.

She pulled back, wishing now she'd put on a robe. She was already bare to him physically, and now he wanted her to bare herself emotionally to him and risk his rejection. If he rejected her, she wasn't sure if she would recover. Icy fear wrapped itself around her heart at the thought of him walking out the door, never to return.

"Does this have something to do with the things I found in your nightstand drawer?"

She coughed.

How did she tell the man she loved that all her sexual desires ran to the dark and painful without scaring him off? That the rough punishment he thought he'd given her in the kitchen was just a taste of what she needed from him? What she wanted. What she desired. She had learned through many adventurous nights that only a small percentage of men wanted to walk the fine line of her desires. They were either too much like Boy Scouts to provide the sexual domination she craved or were just plain mean and cared nothing for her pleasure, only her pain.

"You don't understand," she choked out over the

lump in her throat.

"Then tell me. You might be surprised at my reaction. I'm no longer the scrawny kid you left behind."

Carli searched anxiously for the meaning of his words as he caressed her shoulder. His touch was soothing and warm. "I'm a hardened man who has experienced an adventurous life so far. Nothing you say could shock me."

Carli shook with anticipation as well as a good dose of fear.

"Aidan, when I was nineteen, I didn't understand what I needed and definitely couldn't tell you. How does one kid tell another that she craved sexual domination with a healthy dose of pain? That the sex we engaged in wasn't rough enough?"

She turned away, afraid to look at his eyes, knowing that his revulsion would be evident despite his words. She'd come this far. She might as well keep going. She took a deep breath and continued.

"It's more than me just dipping my toe into adventurous sex now and again. This is a lifestyle for me. Something I need. The one aspect of my life where I can let go and give up control to another."

"Was that really so hard, baby? I already suspected the depth of your need, just based on your reactions to me today. But more than anything, I needed to hear you say it. You needed to say it." He slid his hand down her back, cupping her ass. "When you came back for me, what were you going to do? Tell me what you wanted, or go on as if it was never quite enough to satisfy you?"

"I couldn't have told you then; I was still too

scared. I didn't understand what was wrong with me."

He let go of her ass and delivered a stinging blow to one cheek with his flat palm. "Wrong answer. We can't be together if you aren't willing to tell me the whole truth." He spanked her bottom again, this time a little harder. The bite of pain coursed through her bottom and went straight to her pussy.

"If you continue to lie to me, I will be forced to punish you. And by the way, there's absolutely nothing wrong with you."

Excitement surged through her veins. *Is he saying what I think he's saying?*

"Don't move. I'll be right back."

Chapter Six

Aidan hurried through the living room to her bedroom to gather a few tools. Tonight he would show her he was more than capable of fulfilling all of her wild desires. Hell, his desires, too. It had always been more important to him to control his woman's pleasure, thereby heightening both of their orgasms. But more importantly, it was the gift of submission that he treasured above all else. Knowing that a sub trusted him to give them both what they needed and wanted fueled his control. The problem for him had always been that the one and only woman he ever truly wanted to control was the one woman he thought he couldn't.

Until now.

Now, she waited for him on the balcony with her lush body bared to all, just waiting for him to make his demands. He shuddered as a shiver of anticipation traveled down his spine, his dick so hard he thought it might burst. He had never wanted a woman as much as he wanted her.

Tonight he would bring her to such heights of pleasure there would be no doubt how much he cared for her.

When he returned, Carli was rooted in the same

spot. She bit the corner of her lip, showing eagerness with a touch of fear of the unknown. Good, he needed her to wonder. With her body highlighted by the light of the moon, the moisture on her sex glistened like the stars. The anticipation of what was coming next had begun to prepare her body for his.

"Aidan, we should go inside. Someone might see us." Her tongue darted, nervously moistening her lips. Oh, the ideas he had for that mouth.

"Wasn't that the idea when you came out here naked, looking for me?" He offered her a slow, wicked smile. "No, you will stay right there as I commanded." He spoke with cool authority. "I want you right here."

She watched nervously as he leaned down to the table where he had deposited her toy bag. Reaching in, he pulled out the soft, black, Japanese bondage rope she had purchased months ago but never had the opportunity to use. Her eyes widened at the possibilities of what was to come next. She was so hot that the heat from her pussy made her take a step back.

"Where are you going, Carli?" He grabbed her around the waist and roughly hauled her up against his body. Nibbling kisses along her neck and shoulder, he delved his fingers between the juicy folds of her sex. "Ah, so wet."

She shuddered as he slipped two thick fingers in her channel while his thumb circled her clit. As he continued his onslaught of biting her sensitive flesh and finger-fucking her, an orgasm began to build. She bucked her hips as it drew near, urging him to bring her to completion.

Aidan suddenly withdrew his hand from her pussy, halting her impending eruption. Her body bucked in protest, a whimper escaping her lips.

"You are not allowed to come yet, baby."

She moaned in disapproval, and before she realized what he intended to do, he had bound both of her wrists with the rope and carried her over to a small table. He pushed her onto its top, and when her bare belly connected with the cool wood, she breathed in sharply in shock. He tied both of her wrists to the legs of the table and then proceeded to strap her ankles down. She was left face down with her ass and cunt at the perfect level for his cock. When he spread her cheeks, she knew he was inspecting the tight hole he had fingered earlier.

"You want me to fuck you in the ass, don't you, baby?"

She didn't answer. She couldn't. Her heart was thumping so wildly her lungs tightened in response. It was all she could do to take in air.

"Soon, very soon, I will have my dick in your ass so deep you will beg for mercy."

He walked around to the front of the table. When she looked up, she was in perfect alignment with his crotch. He unbuttoned the tight jeans, and it sprang free, bobbing an inch from her lips.

She opened her mouth, eagerly awaiting his permission to taste him. He pushed forward just enough to bring the deep plum-colored head flush against her lips. The velvety smooth skin was so hot she needed to touch him. Wanted to grip his cock and force it in her mouth. She struggled with her bonds. She was completely helpless and would have to wait until he gave her permission to do as he pleased.

A rumble sounded in his chest as he chuckled over her ineffective attempts. He stepped back a few inches, taking himself in hand. Watching him pump his own shaft while she watched just out of reach was agonizing. Her heartbeat pulsed in her clit as she thought she might come from the beautiful sight before her. When a pearl of liquid appeared on the tip, a strangled moan sounded in her throat.

"What, Carli? Did you say something?"

She shook her head.

"Tell me, baby. Tell me what you need."

His pace quickened on his cock as she gave in to his mastery. Her final doubts dissipated as her thoughts were consumed with sensations and a warm glow throughout her.

"Please, Aidan, please let me taste it. Let me have your cock. Please." His hands stilled as he leaned forward.

"Lick it with your tongue. Swirl it around the head."

She immediately complied, laving the tip of his cock with fervor. Tasting the salty pre-come dripping from his slit. He growled with pleasure and pumped his hips, sliding his cock into her mouth. She suckled him deeply as she continued flickering her tongue along the length of his hot member.

Pushing his hips closer to her mouth, he forced her to take his entire length to the back of her throat. As he slid his cock out, she gently scraped him with her teeth. He rewarded her by sinking his entire length in and out. Her body writhed on the table as she frantically searched for a way to rub her own clit against the hard surface. The blood rushing through the veins of his cock pulsed against her tongue. His orgasm neared, but instead of filling her mouth with his hot semen as she hoped, he abruptly pulled out.

"Aidan, please—please fuck me, now!"

Her body was on fire as she fought with her restraints. Helpless to ease the ache in her pussy. Moving around the table, he positioned the head of his cock against the lips of her cunt.

"Aidan, I can't stand it. Please fuck me hard. Now!" She pushed her hips back as much as her bonds would allow, causing his dick to sink marginally into her opening.

With one slow, agonizing thrust, he sank his cock to the hilt in her hot, gripping pussy. His breath clogged in his throat at the sensation of her muscles clamping down on his dick. He was so close to losing it; he had to be careful, or he wouldn't be able to last long enough to take her ass. And oh, how he wanted to spear her backside with his thick dick. He wanted to hear her screams of pleasure as she fought against the pleasure-pain he would give her. Reaching down, without removing his swollen cock, he grabbed the tube of lubricant he needed.

Squeezing a good amount on his fingers, he eased them between the cheeks of her bottom, spreading the lubricant around the tight hole. She gasped at the initial touch of his fingers to her neglected entrance. Slipping two fingers inside her anus, he began pumping his cock and fingers in the same rhythm.

As his rhythm built, so did his rising orgasm.

When he thought they were both about to come, he pulled completely out.

"No, Aidan. Please don't stop. So close. Need to come," she panted, her words coming out in short gasps.

"You will, baby, but not until I fuck my beautiful submissive's ass." Her body jerked at the word "submissive." "That's right, Carli. Submissive, that's what you are." He began working his thick head against the tight entrance. As her backside slowly yielded, he slid his cock in to the hilt.

"That's it, baby. Take the whole thing." Her ass was so tight he was going to blow any second. She whimpered as she tried to push back. "Call me what you want to call me. Now, dammit!"

"Harder, Master, harder." Finally, she had succumbed.

"That's right, baby. You're mine. Now. Don't even think about leaving me again."

As she begged, he pumped as hard as he could knowing the friction gave her as much pain as pleasure. Her ass clenched on his flesh, driving him closer to the edge.

"More," she cried out. "Please, Sir, harder."

Aidan explored the lines of her back before he tightened his hands on her waist, pulling her roughly onto his shaft. She screamed when she came, her body and muscles quivering around his cock. As her orgasm continued, he kept pumping until his own orgasm burst free, and he shot his load of hot semen in her gripping ass. His cock pulsed inside her as his hips continued to thrust through all the aftershocks of his release.

A long time later, he eased from her body. Barely able to stand, he quickly untied her bonds and scooped her into his arms and carried her back to the bedroom and deposited her on the bed. He retrieved a warm, wet cloth from her bathroom and began to bathe her body. She mumbled something he couldn't understand into the pillow with a sleepy voice.

"Carli, look at me."

She slowly rolled toward him with a shy expression on her face. Her cheeks were flushed and glowing, her hair a wild mass of curls across the pillow. She looked more beautiful to him than ever before.

"I love you. I always have. You belong to me." He absently roamed his hands over the curve of her hip. "Will you marry me this time?" Her look of shock surprised him. Before she could respond, he went on. "I'll expect you to wear my collar as well as my ring, and in bed you will submit to every desire and whim I have with total obedience."

"But outside the bedroom nothing changes?" she asked.

"No, you're still tough, strong Carli, kick-ass investigator. Wife, lover, and one day mother."

Her eyes moistened. She couldn't believe he still wanted her after learning how far she needed him to go. Her pussy tingled with anticipation, knowing he desired to dominate her the way she needed.

"Yes, I'll marry you. I'll be your wife, submissive, and someday mother to your children." She laughed as tears of happiness fell from her eyes.

He reached over and tweaked her nipples playfully as she bit his shoulder. When he smacked her bottom, she wondered how he felt about sharing.

Cupid's Captive
Reese Gabriel

John Cupid hated Valentine's Day almost as much as he hated his name. As a child, he'd been forced to endure endless teasing, and even now people kept at it, acting like he was supposed to be some kind of incarnation of the cherubic god of love.

Love...

John had no more use for it than he did for the holiday. Lust was the only thing one could quantify, and that was far too fickle to control. Being a lawyer, he knew enough to get everything in writing—including the sexual likes and dislikes of his partners.

His own interests tended towards bondage and domination. He was a sexual master, and he liked his women pliant, obedient, and submissive. John gave the orders in bed, and all his naughty, consenting girls got sore bottoms.

Hell, even the good girls got them.

There were no shortage of applicants, due to John's natural charm and good looks. He kept things light, no strings attached, no problems down the line. It was a good system, and tonight he had a hot new prospect lined up: a perky PR executive he'd met at a club last week.

Unfortunately, there are situations one can't get out of in life, and when his partner at the small law firm they co-ran came to him practically begging him to take his little sister out for Valentine's Day, he could see his hot night with Marilee flying out the window.

"John," implored the wiry, lean-faced Carl Hayes. "How often do I ask for personal favors? Steffy is on her college break, and my folks specifically asked me to keep her out of trouble, especially on Valentine's Day. God knows what a pretty, precocious girl like her could get into."

"Why don't you hire a baby sitter?" grumbled John, who was having a hard time seeing Steffy as anything other than the wise-ass seventeen-year-old in pigtails and bright pink sneakers who spent her time listening to music that made a cat fight sound melodic.

Carl shook his head. "She's twenty-one now, John. I can't buy her off with ice cream and lip gloss. If you don't take care of her, she'll go out clubbing. I'd do it myself, but you know I have to meet with that Japanese consortium."

John ran his hand through his thick, dark hair. It was half past four already. "Thanks for the advanced notice."

Carl's expression was pained, his brow pinched. "I can't help it, buddy, she just called me out of the blue."

John sighed. Carl never could stand up to women. "You owe me for this. You do."

"You name your terms." Carl brightened like a man reprieved. "You're the man, John."

"No," he quipped. "I'm the big, fat sucker, born about a minute ago."

John speed-dialed Marilee, his date for the night with the bad news. He had to leave a voice mail. Talk about low class. She'd never speak to him again.

"Aw, it won't be so bad. Trust me, guys will be jealous." Carl winked. "Steffy's all grown up these days."

"You mean all the pimple-faced teenage boys will be jealous," said the thirty-one-year-old John. "Cretins with IQs lower than my golf scores."

"The way you play golf?" Carl grinned. "Einstein's IQ was lower."

"Go on, keep insulting me," John groused. "See if I don't change my mind about watching the brat."

"It's nice to see you, too, Uncle John," trilled a female voice from the door way.

John turned and was immediately stunned by a vision of feminine beauty, not at all the kid he remembered. "Steffy?"

He couldn't help but be dazzled by the picture: green eyes to bring a man to his knees; silky, raven's wing tresses piled seductively on her head; the cute figure so perfectly accentuated in a short, sparkly silver skirt and a matching top, tight across her ample bosom and more than a little revealing of her flat, lightly tanned stomach.

There was a diamond in her belly button, a single piercing on a silver rod, tiny and made of cool steel. Her little pink ears were pierced by silver hoops. Her lips were painted a silvery pink, liquid and glossy; they made him thirst deep within.

"It's been a while, Uncle John." She gave him a hug. The warmth and energy of her was overpowering. This was a woman's body now, molded, instinctively seeking to fit with a male's.

John broke the connection short. Shit, he was getting a hard-on.

"You look good," she said, her voice a bit too sultry for comfort.

And you look like a goddess, he wanted to reply.

"He's had a lot of cosmetic surgery, sis," Carl piped up. "Don't let him fool you."

"He doesn't need it, big brother," she said, looking John in the eye. "Never will."

John's pulse kicked up a notch. Was she flirting with him?

"Oh, great." Carl rolled his eyes. "Just what I need. Someone else pumping up John's ego. I can barely work with him now."

Carl gave Steffy a kiss on the cheek. "Oh, well. Gotta run. You mind your manners and do what Uncle John tells you."

A shiver went down John's spine as he thought of the young woman complying with some of the very X-rated commands on his mind at the moment. She was certainly old enough, though probably not submissive.

Anyway, she was off limits. Too young and practically family to boot. She called him uncle, for crying out loud.

"So...you ready for a night out with the brat?" she said after Carl was gone. She was smiling slanted, eyes challenging.

"I am sorry you overheard that," John said.

"I'm not," she replied, her emerald eyes dancing, full lips moving into a pout. "I like being a brat."

The blood filled John's cock. Steffy was appealing to him at a visceral level. Did she realize just what she was messing with here? Brats had a special place in the world of dominance and submission. They were women who taunted strong men, crossing the line in hopes of being dragged across the knee, pretty little skirts flipped up and panties pulled down for stinging erotic punishment...and whatever followed naturally.

John cleared his throat. "We should...um...get going. Are you hungry?"

She licked her lips. "For food?"

John frowned, ignoring the innuendo. "I know a place nearby, they have burgers and stuff."

She rolled her eyes, not unlike her brother. "I'm a little old for *burgers and stuff,* don't you think?"

"Fine," he said, his temper shortening by the moment. "A steakhouse, then. We'll take my car."

"Whatever you say, Uncle John." She walked in front of him, her ass swaying.

"Does your family approve of you dressing that way?" he asked when they got in the car.

She settled herself into the bucket seat of his English roadster, her legs slightly parted. The skirt rode high on her thighs. "I'm an adult. It's no one's business. Don't tell me you're going to get uptight on me."

He tried to keep his eyes on the road and off Steffy, her belly and ripe breasts, her mile long legs. Talk about blossoming overnight...

"I don't care one way or the other. Just curious."

She opened her legs a little further. Vamp. "Really? Most guys I run across care quite a lot."

"I'm sure they do. I imagine you put quite a lot of ideas in their heads."

John could have kicked himself for letting the conversation go down this road, but it was too late.

Not surprisingly, Steffy pounced. "What about you? Do I put ideas in your mind?"

Time to shut this down fast...

"Not really. I still think of you as a kid, mostly."

"You do?" Her voice was light and playful, but she was all business. That college she'd been at must have taught some interesting things.

"That's funny," she added. "Because that rocket in your pants says otherwise."

John nearly slammed into the car in front of them at the next traffic light. "Young lady, you will refrain from ever speaking to me like that again, is that clear?"

He glared at her. She was biting her lower lip, suppressing a smile, taunting him...but into what exactly?

"Yes, Sir," she rasped.

His cock ached, desperate to be called into play. Why in bloody hell did she have to call him *sir*? She might as well strip naked and throw herself at him.

He had half a mind to dump her off somewhere, but he couldn't do that. He was the adult here, the older adult, and he had to maintain control. "Let's just talk about something else. How do you like school?"

"It's lame." She propped her elbow on the door, palm on her chin. She was adorable, mischievous...practically begging to be taken in hand. But she didn't even know what BDSM was—did she?

"There must be something good about it..."

"I went to a frat party last week and did a beer bong. Then some guys did Jell-O shots off me and my best girl friend."

"Jell-O shots?" He was afraid to ask.

"That's when you lay a girl out, Uncle John, naked or close to it." Her eyes were afire; the minx was trying to get him worked up. "And you eat squares of Jell-O off her stomach, made out of liquor."

"Sounds real educational."

"That's not all we do," she said throatily.

"Don't tell me...you sip champagne from ladies' slippers?"

"Huh?" She laughed at the archaic reference. "No. We let the boys tie us up. Then they do what they want with us."

John's chest seized like a fist. He was instantly jealous. What would a boy know about bondage? They wouldn't know what to do with Steffy...naked...helpless.

"That can be a risky proposition," he said. "Especially if alcohol is involved."

"I like to take chances," she said.

Typical. The Myth of Invulnerability...the disease of every twenty-one-year-old.

"You can wind up dead taking chances."

"Why?" she asked. "Do you know anything about bondage?"

"We're almost to the restaurant," he evaded. "This isn't the time to talk."

"Why? Do I have to get ready to jump out or something?"

"No, you don't. Damn, you're even more of a smart-ass than I remember."

"Quite a compliment coming from you, Uncle John."

"Don't call me that anymore," he said.

She looked at him for a moment. He gripped the wheel, avoiding eye contact like the plague.

"John..." She said it in a whisper, trying it out.

"I'm beginning to think dinner's a bad idea," he announced.

"You want to go somewhere else instead, John? Somewhere more private?"

"Private, yes. With you, no."

"I know all about your secret," she declared out of the blue.

"I don't have secrets."

"Sure you do. You're a Dom."

He pulled into the parking lot of Carolyn's Steak House, wishing he were anywhere else on Earth. Finding a spot out of the light, he said, "We need to talk."

"You said it wasn't the time."

"I changed my mind."

"Do you really want to talk?" She reached for his erection.

"Yes." He grabbed her wrist. "I do."

"You're strong," she marveled.

He put her hand on her lap, out of harm's way. "I don't know what game this is, or what you think you're doing, but Carl is my friend, and I would never—"

"I have no panties on, John. You can check. I'm naked underneath...for you."

"You're old enough to be my daughter," he snapped.

She gave him a look. "No, I'm not. Unless you had a kid when you were, like, ten."

"Just tell me where to take you," he said. "I'll drive you. Right now."

"Your place," she said boldly. "I bet you have a lot of toys in your bedroom. I'm a real bad girl, John; I need punishment."

"You're barking up the wrong tree. I'm not into that stuff."

"Sure you are. I overheard my brother and you talking one time, about someone named Sherry..."

Sherry...shit. His little blonde slave girl from a few years ago. She was married to a doctor, but once a week like clockwork she crawled to John, a play collar on her neck. The way she whimpered and begged and climaxed got to John in a major way. It was one of the few times he almost tipped the balance over into obsession. He'd talked to Carl about it at the time, looking for some advice.

Luckily, her surgeon husband got a position at a hospital out of state shortly thereafter, ending the problem altogether.

"Things shouldn't be taken out of context, Steffy; that was a complicated situation, and you couldn't have understood it."

Steffy grinned. "You said you couldn't live without her twitching, bound ass, freshly reddened and paddled, stuffed full of your hard dick, pleading for you to come inside her. That seems pretty simple to me."

John winced. He'd no idea she was within earshot at the time.

"Whatever." She feigned indifference, pulling back to her side of the seat. "If you don't want me..."

His cock screamed not to let her go. "You're incredibly beautiful, Steffy, and desirable, too. It's got nothing to do with that."

"Is it that you don't think I'm submissive enough?"

Perceptive girl.

"That's part of it, yes."

"There's only one way to find out. A man needs to teach me."

"Why not your boyfriend? Don't you have one?"

"No. I don't like guys my age. They're babies. I let them play with me, that's all. When someone ties me up, I feel so hot. Sometimes I'll tell a boy to tell me what to do, like he's my master. But it's not the same when you're the one giving the orders, you know?"

"Point taken," he concurred.

Steffy leaned in with all the exuberance of youth. Her lips landed on his, so vital and fresh, her eagerness and passion making up for lack of experience. "Will you show me...tonight?" She was practically panting. "I picked you out. I got my brother to get you to take me out. He doesn't even realize how I manipulated him, calling the last minute when I knew he was busy, and then planting the suggestion of you as a companion for me."

John could believe that. His partner Carl was a brilliant legal mind who could find his way around the most hostile courtroom, but give him some personal situation to deal with and he was all thumbs.

"What is it you expect me to show you, Stephanie?"

"How to submit. I want to know if it's in me. If it's something I'd enjoy."

John knew if he didn't do this for her, she would keep experimenting with the wrong people. She might end up in a very bad situation. There wasn't a choice here, although he was not sure the results were going to be to anyone's liking. He was liable to lose a friend...his best friend.

"If you truly want submission, Stephanie, you must begin with obedience. Ninety-nine percent of this stuff isn't sexual at all."

"I...understand," she said, though clearly she didn't.

"You'll do everything I instruct, beginning with dinner. You'll conduct yourself as a disciplined young lady—good posture, please and thank you, no displays to draw attention to yourself."

"Yes. Can I call you *Sir*?"

"You may." So much for this being ninety-nine percent nonsexual. He was ready to burst and they had barely touched each other.

"Thank you, Sir," she said coyly.

"Recline your seat," he ordered.

The tiny motor whirred until she was nearly horizontal. John allowed himself to feel her bare belly. Her skin was smooth as silk, taut as a drum. "Are you wet?" he asked her.

"Sopping wet, Sir." A smile curled her lips, a mix of pride and wonder.

"Show me."

She lifted her bottom, shimmying the skirt up past her full hips to her narrow waist. Her pussy lips were pink and glistening and swollen. He slipped a finger inside her, just past the delicate crack. Stephanie let out a moan.

"Oh, Sir..."

"Move," he commanded. "Against my finger. Make yourself come."

"Yes, Sir." She lifted her hips, an athletic arch, hot and eager. She wanted it pure and raw and now...a finger, a cock, whatever was available.

Her teeth chattered. She was already climaxing. He'd never seen a girl this quick, this responsive. Her face was locked in sheer pleasure, eyes shut tight against the world. A man would have to move fast to stay on top of this one; she was like lightning in a jar.

And he was about to unscrew the top.

"I want you to take a little pain, Steffy."

She screamed out as he pinched her nipple through the sequined top. The mild sensation rode her to a fresh orgasm, bucking, wild enough to shake the car.

"Omigod, omigod, omifuckingod..."

He let her ride it out, then brought her back down, keeping control the whole time. Her toes were still curled as she collapsed back against the seat, her body covered in sweat.

"Good girl," he praised, giving her his wet finger to clean.

Steffy popped it in her mouth, sucking with unbridled enthusiasm, her eyes alit with puppyish devotion.

"Can I do something for you now?" she said.

He shook his head. "I will tell you what to do and when."

Her voice held obvious awe. "Yes, Sir."

"So are you ready?" he asked. "For steak, I mean?"

"Yes, please, Sir." She was in that post-orgasmic phase, soft and complaint. He knew it would pass quickly, especially without any kind of corporal discipline as a reinforcement.

Sure enough, on the way in, she surreptitiously pinched his bottom, back in full brat mode.

"I'm sorry, I couldn't help myself," was her coquettish reply.

He took her by the arm. "I warned you about your behavior, young lady. Later there will be punishment."

"What kind of punishment?" she asked after they were seated at a small, intimate table in the corner, complete with candlelight.

"Too much curiosity is not becoming in a submissive female," he replied, spreading his napkin in his lap.

"What, do you have a paddle or something?"

"Or something," he replied.

"Please, tell me." She was wheedling like a child. "Please, Sir?"

He decided to give her what she wanted. "First you'll strip naked. Then you will stand against the wall, holding three coins in place, one each with your nipples and one with your nose. After a half hour or so, ass exposed, waiting, you will be given a dozen strokes with a riding crop. It will leave welts on your ass. After that, more time to think. Following this, you'll be on your knees, you can guess what for. If at any time during punishment you should happen to drop the coins, by the way, we start over."

"Oh."

"Still feel like you want a submissive experience?"

She had her lower lip in her mouth, wild determination on her face. She could be riding a cock right now for all her sexual focus and intensity. "If you only knew, Sir."

"If it gets to be too much," he told her after he ordered a bottle of red wine and two prime ribs, "you can use a safety word. How about Valentine's Day?"

"What's a safety word?" asked his cute-as-a-button slave wannabe.

John narrowed his gaze. "I knew you shouldn't have been letting boys experiment on you. A safety word is vital to any BDSM experience. It's how the sub ends the activity if it's uncomfortable. A Dom will instantly stop what he's doing."

Her eyes twinkled. She wrinkled her nose. "Are you jealous, Sir, of other boys doing things to me?"

"Don't be ridiculous," he growled, trying to cover the nerve she'd just struck. "I just think a girl like you needs a guy, one guy, to look out after you."

Her small foot, sans shoe, found its way to his trouser leg. "Would you look out for me, Sir? If you were my guy?"

"Keep it up, missy, and we'll be addressing your behavior *before* we get to my place."

She pulled her foot back, though she seemed quite pleased with herself for getting a rise out of him. "Yes, Sir."

"I mean it." He let himself get egged on. "I know the owner of this place, and he'd happily let me use his office."

"What would you do to me?" Her eyes were slits, Eve straight out of Eden, gunning for Adam.

The need to corral her, to put her lovingly in her place, was overwhelming. She was a tough customer, though, not nearly as innocent as some of the women he'd known. Sherry was a child in comparison. It wasn't a matter of how much experience Steffy had had, he decided, but something in her character. She was an old BDSM soul, some kind of vixen reborn.

"Ever been whipped with a belt and fucked over a desk?" he inquired.

She raised a brow. "I thought you'd never ask...Sir. Aren't you afraid I'll break, like a piece of china?"

"Your brother would kill me," he shook his head.

She teased him with her big toe, this time right between the legs.

"That's enough, Stephanie."

"Make me stop."

He was on his feet before he could think about it. Events unfolded in a weird slow motion, with pure erotic punch, the two of them lost in their own world. It was a game he'd played a thousand times before but never with this sharpness, this clarity.

"Let's go, little girl."

She stood, obediently enough, though her lips continued to defy. "I'm not that little...you better hope you can handle me."

John put his hand on her back, the contact electric. "This way."

He steered her into the kitchen and made a hard right, exchanging the barest few pleasantries with Tony, the chef, along the way.

He could see the flush on Steffy's cheeks. Was she aroused, embarrassed?

"Does that man know...about you?" Steffy asked as John walked her down the corridor past the store room to the small but serviceable owner's office.

"You mean have I brought other naughty girls here for correction?"

"Yes." She was all over him, trying to undo his shirt.

He spun her about. Using his tie, he secured her wrists behind her back. "This would be a good time," he breathed hotly, "to change your mind...before we get too far into it."

She leaned back against him. Her voice was otherworldly, the most feminine and arousing he'd ever heard. "No, Sir. I want it, please beat me and fuck me."

Who was he to deny such a pretty and determined young lady?

"Over the desk," he ordered. "On your stomach."

"Yes...Sir...," she rasped.

Her voice was magic; ten times more intoxicating than the wine they'd left behind on the table. Would they ever get back to it? Who cared—as long as he had her in his clutches...his partner's naughty, baby sister.

Correction: naughty, yes, but as far from a baby as you could get.

* * * *

Stephanie Hayes was actually doing it. She was bound and captive, in a stranger's office, submitting like a slave girl to the dreamy, tall, dark and handsome John Cupid. The man she'd had a crush on for as long as she could remember. John had never noticed her before, but there was no ignoring her desires now...or his.

She had been just eighteen when she overheard John telling her brother about his sex slave, Sherry. The way he talked, the things he was describing had awakened sensations deep inside the virgin Steffy. Before long, she was fantasizing about being in Sherry's place, stripped naked, forced to obey...and submit.

She called him Master in her dreams. She wore his collar, and she serviced him for his pleasure. She was his property, and he exercised tight, loving control. She was whipped when she misbehaved, and for rewards she was allowed to suck his cock or spend time with him. She was like a little pet, owned, content. Happy...and strangely free.

For the better part of two years, she thought it would never be real. Why would John want a kid for a slave, least of all his partner's baby sister? But the past year at college had begun to convince her. All of a sudden, her body developed this life of its own. She met some guys and a few girls, too, more than willing to help her develop her wild streak.

She lost her virginity, backed off the studying and started to really live. The more she experienced, the more she knew she wanted John. She didn't dare tell a living soul. Everyone would tell her she was a fool. Too young to know what she wanted and certainly too young for a man like Cupid.

But she'd done research. Age differences weren't that unusual in BDSM relationships. If the chemistry was right, the rest took care of itself.

Steffy knew she'd have to prove herself. John was a practical man, skeptical. Then she'd have to work on everyone else. If she won him over, though, the rest would come easy—including dealing with her brother.

Because if there was one thing Stephanie knew about John Cupid, it was this: When he wanted something, he let nothing stand in his way. At the moment, he wanted her. Over the desk...

"How much will it hurt?" she asked, bent at the waist over the smooth edge, her cheek against the desk, her hands secured behind her back.

The desk was aluminum. She felt the cold, hard metal against her bare midriff. She'd worn the right outfit. From first glance she had him...putty in her hands.

"I won't draw tears, Steffy, you're a novice. But it won't be fun sitting down for a while."

She squirmed as he lifted her skirt.

"Your pussy is incredible," he said. "Your ass is perfect."

She wriggled it for him. "Thank you, Sir. I aim to please you."

"You say you've never had any kind of corporal punishment before?"

"No, Sir." She tingled as he touched her posterior, getting the lay of the land.

"I want you to count," he said. "We're going to ten."

"Yes, Sir." She craned her neck to see him; he was undoing his belt.

"Eyes forward, girl." He snapped his fingers.

A hot blade went through her belly as he chastised her. "Yes, Sir."

Obeying him made her wetter still. She could feel the fluids dripping down her thigh. It must have made for quite a view.

She gasped at the sound of leather, whistling in the air. He was testing the belt. If intimidation was his intent, it was working. Steffy pressed her cheek to the desk, suddenly feeling very small and female. Was it too late to beg?

The belt hit like greased lightning, an efficient blow across the meat of her buttocks. She couldn't help but yelp, a small, high-pitched sound. "One!" she cried, fists clenching and unclenching.

Her reaction did not please him. "Contain yourself, Steffy; this is nothing."

"Y—yes, Sir."

He whipped her again.

"T—two." She grimaced.

The third blow was to the tops of her thighs. It hurt much worse. She did a little dance, one foot to the other. "Three!"

He lashed out, admonishing her. "Hold still."

"F—four."

"No, that last one doesn't count," he informed her. "That was extra for moving around so much."

Steffy whimpered. "Yes, Sir."

She concentrated on standing very still for the next two. "Five," she stammered. "Six."

"Good girl." He patted her ass. "You're learning."

"Th—thank you, Sir." She winced. The light touch had the effect of magnifying her pain a hundredfold.

He pushed a finger deep inside her well-lubricated canal. "Open," he ordered.

She spread her legs...on command. The idea fascinated and enveloped her. She was in bondage, a man's plaything.

Relentless, he hooked a finger up, going to work on her clitoris. "Are you ready for the last four?"

"I...yes...no...I don't know."

"You have to beg for it, girl. You have to surrender to it, completely."

Something inside her resisted. She'd already asked him to beat and fuck her, why make her do it another time? She knew the answer, of course. He was doing it because he could. Besides, that was only theoretical, and this was real. She would actually be seeking out her own punishment.

He brought her to the edge of orgasm and left her hanging.

"I need to come," she wheedled.

"No. You need to finish getting your whipping."

She made a hissing noise. "It's not fair..."

John stepped back and struck her three times, fast and hard. "Those," he said, "do not count either."

Steffy's pussy pulsed, helpless, completely out of her control...stuck in lockdown. Her ass was on fire. She kept on twitching like he was still hitting her. At last, she was seeing it: what a dominant man could do and how a female could be completely overcome, to her own torment and delight.

"Please, tell me what you want..." She scarcely recognized her own voice, thin and haunted and hot as desert wind.

"You already know," he said, imperious and unbending as steel.

She did know, and she saw that she had no choice. "Please, Sir, finish my beating?"

"You may resume the count." He let loose, striking her true.

"Yes, Sir...seven...," she grunted. "Eight."

He paused with two to go. His finger found her clit again. "Come," he commanded.

She exploded at the sound of his voice, rubbing her body, humping the desk like a wild animal and swearing up a storm. Abruptly he removed his finger and struck her, once, twice more.

The whipping melded with the orgasm. She actually stuck her ass in the air. Was she counting? She couldn't hear her voice.

"M—more, please, Sir?"

He went on past ten. To what number she didn't know; she was too far gone in her latest climax. It was an all-over orgasm, a total body orgasm or maybe an out-of-body one. At a certain point in the middle of the explosive crashing, she heard herself screaming for his cock to slam itself home, an extension of his discipline.

Luckily, he thought to put a condom on. In her current state of mind, she never would have asked. She'd have to kid him later about walking around with rubbers all the time, being prepared like a perverted Boy Scout. Or had he been planning on some hot date with somebody else tonight before she came along?

His cock slid into her canal with ease. She was more than ready, hot and wet and pulsing. "Yes, oh, yes." She encouraged her own invasion. "Do it to me, use me..."

Her words had the desired effect. He grabbed her waist in an iron grip and slammed himself in to the hilt. Immediately he pulled back and did it again. By the third time, she was ready to peak all over again.

"Come inside me, fucking come inside me, lover," she cried.

"I'll give the orders." He slapped her throbbing buttocks, bringing back every single blow of the belt.

She moaned, slipping into a space somewhere to the outside of normal consciousness. She looked down at her own body, saw what was happening to her, just as she saw where it was going.

"Master," she gasped, using the title entirely without permission. "Your slave surrenders to you. She...she loves you."

Always has, she might have added, though again, the words wouldn't have been believed from the mouth of a twenty-one-year-old.

Oh, yes, she'd known it would be this good. The others, the boys at school were so scared of her, awed by her beauty, but John, he knew what to do with her.

John stopped in midstroke.

Had she done something wrong, said something wrong?

Of course you did, you dolt. Never tell a man you love him, not right off. That was the most basic rule...

"Sir?"

He withdrew his cock. "I'm sorry, Stephanie. It shouldn't have gone this far. It's all my fault."

She felt him releasing the tie on her wrists. "But..."

"We can still have dinner if you like."

Have dinner...after this? Was he serious?

Steffy dropped to her knees, all semblance of pride gone. "I'll do anything..."

"Stephanie, don't." There was a trace of annoyance in his voice, even pity.

She couldn't hold back the tears. He tried to help her to her feet, she pushed him away. "Leave me alone, you bastard."

"Steffy, be reasonable. You can't stay here."

"I'll stay where I like; you don't own me."

What a stupid little fool she'd been, a lovesick puppy, blind to the reality of a hard-nosed, hard-hearted man. Why would he want her? She was young and silly. She scooted back on her heels.

John spoke harshly, appealing to something deep inside her. "Stephanie, stop this nonsense. Get up now!"

She obeyed in spite of herself.

He handed her a tissue to wipe her nose. "Go in there," he ordered, pointing to a small bathroom adjacent to the office. "Clean yourself up, and I'll take you back to your brother's."

"Yes," she said, omitting the *Sir*.

She closed the door, deeply ashamed, highly confused. What did he want from her? He was ordering her about like a slave girl; she was doing what she was told. He'd been attracted to her enough to put his cock in her. So she happened to love him. Did that mean they couldn't have any kind of relationship?

"Can we at least talk about it?" she asked when she came out, as together as she could arrange herself with a small sink and mirror and the few items in her purse.

"No," he said, stone-faced.

She fell twice as much in love with him with that one look, so powerful and angry...but still a teddy bear underneath. Damn, did it ever suck being a woman, totally dependent on hormones.

He left a lot of money on the table for the meal they didn't eat; such a waste, that nice bottle of wine.

They walked back to the car without a word exchanged.

"I don't suppose another beating would make things right?" she quipped, sitting herself gingerly on the leather seat.

"Time will make it right," he said, not a trace of humor. "And distance."

He was brushing her off.

"You're a real prick," she shot back, not feeling particularly mature anymore.

The silence thickened to a dark soup.

"You're not such a big man," she said petulantly, the car just a block from Carl's house, where he lived with three golden retrievers and a Siamese cat named Ginger. "You have feelings you don't talk about. I think you're a scared little boy on the inside."

His gaze narrowed. It was the first time she'd seen him even a little perturbed. "Thanks for the unsolicited opinion of a brat, Stephanie; a spoiled girl who doesn't like it when she can't get what she wants."

Wow, she thought. I've hit a raw nerve and he's just striking back, taking pot shots.

"Tell me, Uncle John." She went for broke. "Why don't you have real relationships? Are you gay?"

He smiled, quite superior. "You want a reaction out of me pretty bad, don't you, young lady?"

"Yes," she replied, summoning every bit of courage in her young body. "I do, Master."

Something flashed across his eyes. She couldn't read it. "I'm not your master," he said.

"You could be," she retorted. "If you wanted."

"You don't know what you're talking about. What did you do, read some shit on the Internet? Women twice your age don't know what they want; you couldn't possibly."

"What if I do?" She flipped back her hair. "Are you man enough to handle me, or don't you know what you want either?"

John frowned and sped up the car. Straight past her brother's house.

Mission accomplished.

"You can wipe that smirk off your face, young lady," he informed her.

"What smirk, Sir?"

"Open the glove compartment," he replied. "There's a vibrator in there."

"Yes, Sir." She fished for it eagerly. It was a small, clear plastic egg. Her pussy contracted at the sight of it.

"Spread your legs wide," he ordered. "Put it inside yourself. Set it on high."

Steffy widened her thighs. Her cunt took the device, buzzing, hungry. She bit at her lower lip and sucked for air.

"Now you're going to be quiet," he told her, "while I do the talking."

"Yes...Master."

He didn't bother to correct her. The first of the orgasms overtook her as he accelerated, taking the on ramp onto the highway. Were they headed somewhere in particular or just driving?

"First of all, missy, you are barking up the wrong tree if you think I'm scared of commitment or some nonsense. I don't believe in love, that's all, and I have plenty of evidence on my side. Prove me wrong, that's what I say. If you think you're in love, that's great. You can feel just as strong at twenty-one as eighty-one, that's your concern. Me, I like sex, I like to play, with lots of different women. Hang around me, and that's what you get, play."

He glanced in her direction. "Pinch your nipples," he decided. "Make it hurt a little."

Steffy writhed on the seat. The touch of her swollen nubs set her off all over again.

"Jeezus," he rasped, low in his throat. "What I could do with you alone for a weekend..."

I'm yours, she longed to say, for a lifetime.

"Like I said, I play with women. I respect them, I'm honest, but I don't commit. I have rules. You already made me break one of them. I have no idea what I'll say to Carl."

"Tell him...you claimed me," she said, breathless.

"I'll do no such thing," he snorted. "Don't you get it, girl? All of this is to show you that you don't want to live with me. In another hour, you'll be begging to get out of this car and out of my life."

"Never," she said stubbornly.

His lips thinned, creases on both sides of his mouth. "Son of a bitch."

He moved to the left-hand lane, accelerating. "You're going to attend to me," he said.

Her mouth watered as he undid his fly. "Oh, God, yes..."

She dropped her head to his lap, greedily pulling his cock from out of his underwear. She kissed the tip of it. "Thank you, thank you, Master."

The vibrator hummed away, continuing to carve away at her will, leaving her a pliant lump of flesh. Beg for release in an hour? No way; she wouldn't even be able to walk by then.

"I haven't done anything like this in ten years," he said, picking up speed. Steffy's heart was racing, faster than the engine. She ducked her head lower, taking the mass of him deep inside her mouth. She wanted him at the back of her throat, she wanted to service and suck, suctioning with her tongue, pleasing him like a good little slave.

He stroked her hair. "You're too good to be true," he said, as if talking to himself.

Her ears perked up; her brain took note. Was that it? Did he not think himself worthy of the gift of another's submission, the offering of her love and not merely her reposited, fleeting lust?

She closed her eyes, giving him what he needed. She felt like she'd done this a thousand times before. His sighs were heartfelt in reply. "Steffy," he said, causing a knot to form in her heart.

It was music to her ears. Up to then, she hadn't known what her name was capable of sounding like.

He erupted easily down her throat, dick throbbing, a volcano, spewing warm, thick semen. She drank every drop, sucking him dry, happily.

The small sports car continued to race like the wind through the night air. She licked his shaft like a puppy with a bone. She kissed the tip of him once again and each of his testicles, too.

"Take out the vibrator," he said.

She removed it, drenched. Her pussy clenched, missing it already. The only thing on her mind, however, was his pleasure. "Was I good, Master?"

His hand settled on her thigh, gentle but possessive, his large fingers spread wide. "Too good," he said, making it sound like a crime.

Steffy let her head rest on his shoulder. "I'm sorry I've been such trouble."

The tears dripping from her eyes were as far from manipulative as you could get. She hoped he understood that. "I'm such a baby," she castigated herself.

"No," he said with surprising vigor. "You're a woman. One of the most grown up I've ever met."

She sniffled. "Thank you."

"And you're no bother to me." His hand slipped around her shoulder. "Do you believe me?"

"Yes." She could stay like this, in his embrace forever.

What was wrong with her that he couldn't love her back?

She was afraid to say anything else and make it all worse.

John exited and turned back for the city.

"I hope you won't be compromised," he said as they neared the house again, "if your brother sees you come in like this."

"He said he wouldn't be back until real late. It's only eleven," she said.

Only eleven? Had everything between them happened in just a few short hours? It wasn't fair. Time wasn't working right. It ought to be pushing them together, giving them a second chance. Wasn't that how it always was in the movies?

Dumb girl. This isn't a movie. This is your life, screwed up as usual.

"Are you going to be all right?" he asked as he dropped her off.

"Me? Hell, yeah."

"Okay." He seemed skeptical. "If you ever want to talk or anything..."

"What for?" She rolled her eyes. "You don't think I was serious, do you, about being in love? I was just playing, Uncle John."

He frowned slightly, those creases appearing around his eyes again. If only this man would talk to her...

"Good night," she said, hopping out of the car. "See you around."

"Yeah...around." He sounded lackluster. Did that reflect a desire never to see her again or was it something else?

She went upstairs to take a shower.

Men were a nuisance, and she planned on not falling in love with any more of them for a long, long time.

Now all she had to do was forget the one she was already in love with...the one who had just broken her heart.

* * * *

"So," Carl asked John the next day, striding innocently into his office. "How did it go last night?"

"It was fine," he answered. Unable to resist, he asked, "Did Steffy say anything?"

"Not a word. You know how they are at that age, though. I think she's after some boy right now. Online. She was still up at two a.m. when I came home."

"What do you mean she's after a boy?"

Carl cocked his head. John cursed himself for reacting so strongly. "I don't know, it's the Internet. You don't look so good, buddy; did you get any sleep?"

"The brat wore me out, that's all," he said, trying to divert attention from his jealous reaction of a moment ago. "You really owe me big time, you know."

"I do," he agreed. "And I have just the way to pay you off. You know Anita, my travel agent? Well, she has this sister who sounds right up your alley.

Smoking hot body, a little left of center in the bedroom, if you know what I mean, and happily unattached.

"I'm not interested, thank you."

Carl was definitely suspicious now. "You? Not interested? That's like Old Faithful being on strike."

John couldn't figure it out himself. He'd tossed and turned all night. All he could think about was Stephanie. How could a woman that young fire all of his cylinders like that? She had no experience. Hell, she was barely submissive at all. That mouth of hers, that sass, that wasn't going anywhere. In fact, that's one of the things he loved about her.

Scratch that. It was one of the things he *liked* about her.

Like, not love.

"How long is Stephanie in town for?" John wanted to know.

"So it's Stephanie now, is it?" Carl arched a brow. "I guess she's not a gum-chewing teenager in your eyes any more, huh?"

"What's that supposed to mean? She's a beautiful young woman," John snapped. "What, am I supposed to be blind?"

"Hey, take it easy." Carl laughed, a little nervously. "I was just joking with you."

"Maybe it's not a good subject for jokes," said John. "She's your baby sister. You should be thinking about helping her find her way in life. She has a very tender heart. A woman like that will get taken advantage of, not to mention having her heart broken by a lot of callous jerks."

Like me, he thought glumly. *Because I was too stupid, too stubborn to give her a chance. She was offering me something special. Why didn't I take it? Could it be I really am scared?*

It was Carl's turn to be defensive. "She's an adult, like you said. She'll have to learn. We all did. Obviously, I'll take care of her as best I can."

"You and me both," said John.

Carl had his mouth open like he was going to say something but thought better of it. "I've got a deposition to take in a half hour." He excused himself.

"So go. What am I, your keeper?" John was irritable as hell. He should have asked for Steffy's cell phone number. Would she pick up at Carl's house?

She did. On the fifth ring.

His heart swelled, hearing her sleepy, lazy voice. "It's after one," he said. "Shouldn't you be awake by now?"

"What's it to you?" she said.

John ground his teeth, having been put squarely in his place. "Nothing. But maybe I would *like* it to be something."

"Uncle John, I really don't want to play guessing games. If you have anything to say..."

How about 'I love you, Steffy'...would that be so hard?

"I have plenty to say. You can drop that Uncle John thing, for starters. It's highly inaccurate and damned inappropriate under the circumstances."

"I'm going to hang up," she said.

"Don't."

"Why not?"

"Because I said."

"Is that a request or an order?"

"A request."

"I don't do requests, sorry."

John exploded. "Young lady, you are begging for a spanking."

"Really? Maybe I'll go find a man to give me one."

His body tensed. Testosterone surged. There was no turning back. "You will come to my apartment, tonight. 5611 12th Street Northwest. The door will be unlocked. You will close it behind you and strip naked. You will arrive at eight and wait for me in the living room. I expect to find you kneeling by the coffee table...one very sorry little slave girl."

More silence. "Is that what I am? Your slave?"

"I said so, didn't I?"

"I'm not interested in one-night stands," she said. "Is that what this is?"

"Do you have to think so much?" he complained.

"Yes. Answer my question. When you're done with me tonight, when your cock is drained in whatever orifice of mine you choose, will you push me out the door, until you want me again?"

His head pounded. How could a woman be cornering him like this? "This isn't how a submissive behaves," he said.

"It's how I behave, though; take it or leave it."

"What if you're the one who wants to take off afterwards?" He tried to turn the tables. "You have no idea how you'll respond to a real taste of slavery."

"I will be leaving, actually." She confused the hell out of him. "I go back to school in two days. But I want to leave my heart with you. I want it to be yours. I want your chains, John Cupid. I want you to want me so fiercely that you will singe my bottom bright red if I so much as look at another man, even if I'm a thousand miles away. I want your brand on my soul, so I'll breathe only for you, no matter where I am. I want to live for you, John, even as I pursue my own gifts."

Her words overwhelmed him. He'd never heard such a mature way of looking at things. "I don't get it." He tried to pick holes. "You're saying you won't even live with me?"

"Of course I will, when it's time. You'll know me better by then, I'll finish school, we'll decide together what my slavery should look like. It'll be like any other union of souls. You commit ahead of time and then work it out as you go along."

"You know nothing about me..."

"I've known you since I was six."

"Okay, I know nothing about you."

"I'll teach you...the way a slave is supposed to teach her master, showing him who she is and what she needs to be loved and properly owned."

John was wordless, for the first time in his adult life.

"Hello?" she said, her voice soft, melodic...the sweetest sound on the planet.

"Be at my apartment by seven," he said gruffly. "If you're late, you'll answer to me."

"Yes, Master."

He hung up...just in time to avoid saying anything incriminating.

* * * *

Steffy trembled slightly as she saw the numbers in gold above the front door of the building. 5611 12th St. NW was a real place after all...and she was about to perform as a real slave. She flushed heatedly when the doorman appeared to ask her destination.

She stammered the name. John Cupid. He smiled expertly, politely.

How many other young women had he let in for similar purposes? Would he confirm her instructions, make sure she knew to kneel properly, subservient and naked until the master appeared?

Of course not. He was far too professional.

Her pulse raced as she rode the elevator. She wore a simple black dress, nothing underneath, and leather pumps. Was that the proper garb? She'd never done this sort of thing. John hadn't told her what to wear. Apparently he didn't care about clothes, only the body underneath. To that end, she'd taken a long and thorough bath, full of fragrant emollients. Lots of suds to make her tingle. It had been hard not to masturbate. She was so excited thinking of what John would do to her.

She wished she could appear before him in some kind of garment, though, no matter how skimpy. Like most young women, she was all too aware of the imperfections of her body. Mostly she hid them, and men were generally quite pleased with her. Usually she overcompensated with flirtatiousness and a veil of indifference. But this was different. She cared what John thought, desperately so.

Her stomach roiled.

She found his door unlocked. She entered and looked about his apartment. The decor was Spartan, elegantly simple. A black leather couch, a single slate coffee table, a solid steel pole lamp, a single black area rug, thick and soft.

The coffee table...that's where she was supposed to kneel.

There was a blindfold on it. Should she put it on?

Her fingers were numb as she undid the zipper on the back of her dress. She removed it and let it drop to the floor, goose pimples on her clean skin, freshly shaven legs, tight, erect rosebud nipples. She smelled of spring flowers and summer rain...and raw sex.

It was all really true: Steffy was about to put herself in submission to a sexually dominant man.

Her knees gave way in slow motion, of their own accord. She went down, all the way to the floor. The coffee table was right in front of her. She picked up the blindfold, black silk, form-fitting. Her heart pounded as she put it to her eyes, sliding the elastic over her head.

It was a perfect fit. Her world was enveloped by artificial darkness. By her own hand, she'd rendered herself helpless. The fluids of her arousal dripped down her inner thighs. She hungered for a cock; she craved to be pushed to the floor and taken.

Steffy thought about posture. She straightened her back and pressed her buttocks to her heels...waiting.

The clock ticked on the wall, sleek and modern, with two faces, no numbers. Its details were etched in her mind, in the memory of her sighted self.

Where was John, she wondered. Would he be here soon?

Even a minute was torture in this state. It would have been easier and less slavishly humiliating to have been tied down, ankles wide like a wishbone than to be forced into voluntary servitude. After all, what kind of a woman subjected herself to this kind of treatment, willingly going to a man's apartment to arrange herself like a sex doll?

Never once did she think of turning back, though. She had come too far. She had to see this through. She'd taken a chance, sure, but so had John. He'd opened his home to her, made himself vulnerable. She could reject him, she could walk out, and he would be left holding the bag of his sexual desires.

Masters were vulnerable, too...

Anyone was vulnerable whose needs were out of the ordinary.

The waiting ended as suddenly as it began.

"Place your hands behind your neck, lace your fingers," came the voice, at once familiar and strangely alien.

"Master," she gasped. Her arms went into place, the action coming as a reflex, as necessary to her survival and well-being as breathing.

"Stomach in, breasts thrust out."

She presented herself for his pleasure, nipples burning. Where had he come from? Had she missed the sound of the front door, or had he been in the back of the apartment the whole time?

Steffy could hear his breathing. He was right in front of her now. She nearly swooned. Oh, God, he was giving her his cock...

She leaned forward, kissing, licking, ravenous. He made her work for it, teasing, rubbing it over her cheeks. She whimpered, wanting to take it fully inside her mouth.

The cock disappeared. A collar was put on her neck, with a leash. He pushed his hand to her lips. She kissed his knuckles. "Master...I love you, Sir, I missed you..."

Without her eyes, it was all so intense; she was so incredibly dependent. Her other senses were so intense. The smell of musk on his skin, the feel of his knuckles.

"I missed you, too," he said. His fist balled in her hair, painful. He fed her his balls. She bathed them in her saliva, worshipping. They were full and tight. He must have been very ready to come.

Still holding her head captive, he twisted his body around.

He presented his buttocks, lean and hard. She kissed eagerly; there was no degradation in the act but rather joy, pure and proud.

"Lick," he ordered.

Stephanie spread her tongue over her master's ass, smooth skin over taut muscle. She paid him homage, letting him know she did understand slavery, and she was ready to proceed.

Satisfied, he bent her head back. "Slavery isn't a game," he said. "It's playful, it's fun, and it's consensual. But it's very real."

"I really do want to be your girl, Master," said Steffy, speaking with a certainty that only grew with each passing second. "I want you to control my body. I want you to use me, punish me and own me."

"There's a lot you don't know," he said, much gentler than last night and without accusation.

"I beg you to teach me, Master."

"I don't know if I'm ready," he said.

The admission touched her deeply. She wished she could see his face, so she could read the pain and help.

"Master, you don't have to be ready," she said. "You already own me. Just be yourself and that will be enough."

He chuckled. "How did you get to be so wise?"

"You've been helping me grow beyond my years, for a long time now."

"We've barely seen each other in ages, how can that be?"

"Because I've been in love with you since I was a kid, Master."

He pulled her to her feet. His kiss claimed her mouth. She yielded with a moan as he plundered with his tongue. Her sex throbbed. She pushed her body forward, seeking his. He was still dressed. His clothing rubbed her skin, making her feel all the more like his slut and pet.

An impulse rose from within, wickedly indulgent and self-deprecating.

"May I kiss your feet, Master?"

John released her, allowing her to sink to the floor. She pressed her lips to the leather, kissing. At once she pressed her lips and then began to run her tongue up and down, over the surface, cleaning his shoes.

"Lie on your back, girl," he ordered at last.

"Yes, Master." She lowered herself, feeling with her hands. She spread wide, legs far apart as they could go.

"Lift your pussy."

She tensed her buttocks, raising them off the floor.

"I want to whip you," he said.

"Yes, Master." She steeled herself, sensing the importance, not to mention the pain.

"Then I want to fuck you," he declared.

"Yes, Master."

He removed the blindfold from her eyes. "I want your consent. I want to hear the words."

It took just a moment to adjust. The first thing her eyes beheld was him, his steady presence, wanting, needing...loving?

"Master, please whip me," she said without hesitation.

"Whip my pussy," he clarified.

"Yes...my pussy."

The whip sliced through the air. She could hear the thin leather; she could practically feel it already.

"You are so beautiful," he marveled. "Stephanie, what are you doing in my life?"

"I'm here to be whipped." She smiled. "And fucked."

The leather slashed down across her pelvis. She cried out from the pain, collapsing back to the floor.

Adrenaline surged through her, along with a sense of deep pride in enduring this for him.

"Ass up," he ordered.

She resumed her position, teeth gritted, sweat on her forehead.

He struck her again. She moaned in pain, a pain mixed with the sharp, intense pleasure of stimulation across her labia. She'd never felt anything like this in her life. "M—master...what are you doing to me?"

"Training you," he said.

"Y—yes, Master."

He whipped her again. "You are mine."

"I'm yours, Master."

"You will obey me in all things sexual."

"I will, Master."

"You will be my sex slave."

"Oh, yes, Master."

"Tell me what you need, beg to be used."

"Master," she groaned. "Use your slave's pussy."

"Cup your breasts now," he ordered. "Squeeze your nipples."

She did so, even as he began to drop his clothes, draping them over her ankles.

"Yes, Master," she cried in anticipation. "I want it, hot and naked, your body pounding me..."

He fell on top of her, slamming his cock home. He sank his teeth into her neck. She felt the shock waves, a torrent to ride. Holding on, she wrapped her legs around his ass, locking her ankles.

He took hold of her wrists, pinning them down on either side of her head. A winch couldn't free her from that kind of grip.

The soft fur beneath cushioned her pliant body. They were skin to skin, the heat of them communicating volumes. He lowered his head to her breast, trapping the rubbery nipple between his teeth. She writhed beneath him, at once trapped and free.

"You will not come without permission."

Steffy whimpered at his glorious cruelty. "Yes, Master."

"If you do, you will be punished."

"Yes, Master," she breathed. "I will try to obey."

He grinned, making it impossible with his long thrusts and his teasing kisses to her neck.

She moaned, vanquished, her body betraying her shattered will; his plaything, that's all she was.

"M—master," she felt the shock waves overcome her. "I can't...help it."

"Bad girl," he crooned, sounding quite pleased with himself. "You'll definitely pay for this. Remember what I said? About holding the nickels to the wall, with your nose and breasts?"

Did she remember? How could she ever forget?

An explosion came from so deep. She'd never felt so helpless. Orgasms within orgasms, a catapulting into air too thin too breathe.

"You like that idea, don't you, my little angel? Maybe I will fuck you from behind at the same time."

"P—please, Master..."

What was she begging for? She didn't even know. Did she want him to stop or to never stop?

John pulled himself from her pussy, his hard-on intact.

What hope did she have when a man had that kind of self-control?

He moved down her body, and she almost screamed as he put his tongue inside her. No man had ever given her oral pleasure. His hands molded her breasts, every bit of resistance was gone, she'd had a million volts of sexual energy pass through her, and he was intent on delivering a million more.

Death by orgasm; was it possible?

His tongue a little weapon, a devious mini-cock that knew all the places to go; it owned her; he owned her. She didn't know her body could do this. Had he been given some manual she'd missed out on? *The Proper Use and Torment of Stephanie Hayes? Enslaving Steffy For Dummies*?

She begged for mercy, beyond tears, beyond pleading.

She began to laugh, hysterical.

"It's settled," he declared suddenly, taking her in his arms.

"What's...settled?" She could barely get the words out.

His eyes were fierce and playful, depthless and infinite as the sea. "I, John Cupid, am officially smitten with you."

Her heart soared. "Is that all, Master?" she asked coquettishly.

"Wench," he growled.

"Yes?" she teased.

"You want to hear the words, don't you?"

"Please, Sir."

"Fine. I love you."

"You don't have to make it sound like a disease."

"Why not? It's going to get me in enough trouble," John declared.

"I can handle my brother, if that's what you mean."

"It's not Carl I'm worried about; it's me."

"You?" She giggled. "Big, tough John Cupid afraid of a little slave girl?"

"You're not any little slave girl; you're a she-devil. Hell, I think I am going to sponsor you for law school; you'd make mincemeat of any opposing attorney."

"I will keep my debate skills sharp with you alone, thank you very much," she countered.

John rose and quickly scooped her to her feet. He took her straight to his bedroom.

"What about my punishment?" she reminded him.

"That will have to wait."

She could feel his cock, pushing up against her. She wrapped her arms tighter about his neck. "What for, I wonder?"

"Take a wild guess." He tossed her down on his bed, large and comfortable and very masculine with its black bedspread.

She promptly crawled away, toward the head board. "Not tonight, dear, I have a headache.

John pounced, pinning her. "Headache, my ass. You're my sex slave, remember?"

"Oh, yeah." She grinned, reveling in having the sexiest man on the planet on top of her, dominating her. "I forgot."

"This help your memory any?" He sank his cock in with a single stroke.

"Maybe a little."

He withdrew to the tip, palms bracing on either side of her, holding his firm, muscular body above her, just out of reach. "Beg for it."

"I don't think so." She wrinkled her nose, testing.

He smiled, liking the challenge. Very slowly, expertly, he began to tease, giving her just enough of his hot, pulsing shaft to drive her wild, but never enough to satisfy.

"Beg," he said again.

She thrashed her head, defying.

"I can do this all night..."

She didn't doubt him. "This isn't fair, Master."

"It's not supposed to be." He licked her left breast, moistening her hot, smooth skin.

Steffy lifted herself off the bed, trying to pull him inside her.

He gave her nipple a warning chew. "Lie still."

She collapsed, frustrated, defeated. "Please?" she said in a small voice.

"Please what?"

"Please fuck me."

He shook his head. "That isn't close to begging."

"Please?" she mouthed, her voice a faint, hot breath. "Please use your slave?"

"Why?"

"B—because..."

"Not an answer." He took his cock all the way out.

"Because she needs you, Master," she said quickly. "Your slave needs to be owned by your cock. She needs to give you pleasure."

"Who is in control?" he asked.

"You are," she assured.

"You've stopped begging," he noted.

"Please fuck me, Master, come inside me, I am your girl, I am your sex slave. Let my body please you. I'll be a good girl; I'll be your obedient little pet..."

"Damn straight you will." He came down on her, ferocious, teeth gritted. His power put her in utter awe. She'd had no idea a man could desire a woman like this, let alone a woman like her.

"I love you," he declared. "God help me, you are beautiful, intense and intelligent...more than I have a right to ask from the universe."

"But I'm here." She clutched at his upper arms. "I'm real, and I'm not going anywhere."

He inclined his head, letting out a deep guttural groan. His semen released inside her, his penis fully submerged. She clenched her pussy muscles, milking him, taking every dominant drop, savoring every star-swept moment.

John Cupid...having sex with her, making love, calling her his.

They slept together afterwards, front to back, perfectly spooned, his hand circling her waist. He held her firm, tight, possessive.

At one point, she had to go to the bathroom.

"It'll cost you," he said.

She returned to find him lying on his back, hands behind his head on the pillow. What a specimen, she thought, with his hard abdomen and muscled chest slowly rising and falling, his cock half-stiff again, his balls as full and tight as before.

Steffy didn't need to be told what to do.

She crawled onto the bed, between his legs. She began with his calves, delivering tiny kisses. He was hard as a rock by the time she got to his cock.

"I was supposed to do that," she said, with a mock pout.

"You already did," he said with a chuckle.

Hungrily, she buried him between her lips. She took the length of him like a lollipop, the sweetest flavor. It was the perfect ending to a perfect night. An ending that was also a beginning. So much to look forward to, so much to think about. This was like a dream come true, but she wasn't naïve. It would be hard work, anything good was a struggle, but the ends were worth it.

He let her suck for a bit, then he had her mount him, straddling his lean waist, impaling herself. She ran her fingers through her hair, closing her eyes. He told her again how beautiful she was and was she sure she really wanted to be mixed up with him?

Yes, a million times yes.

Her body did the talking.

One more rocking orgasm for the night, mutual and wild, hearts merged, two souls intertwining, yearning to learn more about the other.

They collapsed afterward in a tangle, and this time, it was deeper than sleep...more intense than a dream.

She was happy, fulfilled...Cupid's Captive.

Sexy heroes, sassy heroines, compelling stories… Phaze has what you want to read in eBook and paperback.

Enjoy another taste of award-winning sensual fiction from

fine flickering hungers

by Alessia Brio

WINNER: 2007 EPPIE AWARD - BEST EROTICA

Visit us at Phaze.com for more sizzling stories by renowned authors and rising stars of romance.

Listen To Me

She's standing there—by the window—with her back to the room, silhouetted by the moonlight filtering through the sliding glass doors that lead to the balcony. I'm sure she hears me enter, but she doesn't turn around. Closing the heavy door behind me, I turn the deadbolt, and she flinches to the soft snick of it.

We've planned this, negotiated it, but she's still nervous. I can tell. Although she's perfectly still, I can read the apprehension in the set of her shoulders. A little fear won't hurt. In fact, it'll probably help. I cross the room in four long strides, tossing my shoulder bag on the king-sized bed in passing, and I stand very close to her with my hands clasped behind my back.

Leaning forward so that just my breasts brush against her back, I bury my nose in her hair and inhale deeply. Her thick, dark curls smell like rain—warm, summer rain tinged with the cloying scent of honeysuckle blossoms. I lift her hair away from her neck and whisper into the skin just below her ear, "Listen to me." She shivers to the husky tone of my voice, the sensation of my breath. "Are you ready for this?"

In response, she drops her head back against my shoulder and sighs—half exhalation, half 'Yes'...and all surrender. I smile. It's a devilish little grin, full of the most exquisite potential. Tonight will be well worth the months of waiting.

I grasp each of her arms from where they're folded against her chest and smooth them to her sides. Her neck and shoulders tense, and I take a little time to massage them. Not much, though. I'm impatient for her skin.

When she's relaxed a little bit, I reach around her body to unbutton and remove her blouse. Her creamy skin glows in the silvery light, and she gasps as I nibble on her bare shoulders. My hands continue to disrobe her as my mouth enjoys the salty-sweet taste of her flesh. When her jeans puddle around her ankles, she steps out of them.

"Don't move," I caution, crossing the room to fetch my bag. The zipper is loud against the backdrop of the night, and I pull it very slowly—savoring her fear-tinged curiosity. She starts to turn around, but stops when I say, "No." I extract two items, placing them on the corner of the bed, and grab a third.

Returning to her, I trail the silk scarf across her ass and up her spine. A blush suffuses her skin. I can feel it rather than see it—a slight increase in the surface temperature, a slight shift in her scent. When I drape the scarf over her eyes, she giggles nervously.

"Listen to me. Are you ready for this?" I ask as I fold it over her eyes and knot it at the back of her head.

She just whimpers. The sound of it stokes me,

and I back away from her long enough to undress myself. She cocks her head to the side, listening—her other senses beginning to heighten due to the loss of vision. I can tell she's fighting the urge to turn but resists.

Grabbing the items I'd taken from my bag, I stand before her and hold them under her nose. "What do you smell, kitten?"

She inhales, then groans softly, but doesn't speak. I grasp one wrist and buckle a black leather cuff around it. "Are you ready for this?"

"Please," she whispers, offering her other wrist to be cuffed. "Please."

I push her hand away and press my bare body to hers. Warm, almost feverish, skin greets me from shoulder to thigh. She searches for my mouth—blindly—with her own, but I do not let her catch it. Her desperation amuses me. Her body excites me. Her submission thrills me.

Circling her, I cuff the other wrist and join the two behind her back with a metal clamp. The bonds pull her shoulders back and lift her breasts. Her nipples are taut—eager for my attentions. I lead her toward the sofa, pausing to push the small coffee table out of the way.

She hesitates, then takes the tiniest of steps, hampered by both her lack of vision and inability to balance. When we reach the sofa, I position myself against the back and pull her down so that she's sitting in front of me, between my legs. I can feel the heavy leather cuffs against my bare mons and the wiggle of her fingers when she realizes where her hands rest.

"Nice," I growl into her hair, pulling her backward until she's lying against my chest. Her back arches toward the ceiling, and she turns her head toward mine. This time, I let her kiss me—and the taste of her lips coupled with the movement of her fingers brings a surge of wetness. She feels it, too, and chuckles softly into my mouth.

Breaking the kiss—lest I get lost in the pleasure she's giving me—I snake my arms through hers and wrap them around her waist to caress her skin. She holds her breath, waiting for me to move toward either her nipples or her pussy. I do both—abruptly—and she voices her appreciation.

"Hush!" I scold, giving her pussy a slap and twisting a nipple. "You'll wake the neighbors." She doesn't hear me, though. She's in the zone.

With her feet planted on the floor, she pushes her hips upward in search of my hand, lifting her ass off the sofa and crushing my chest with her shoulders. I release her nipple and allow both hands to settle between her legs, one focusing on her clit while the other dips deeper to slide a couple fingers into her wet cunt.

The scent of her arousal permeates my mind, and I want to taste her—to drive her crazy with my tongue. But that's too easy, too fast—for both of us. This rendezvous requires at least a little patience. Plus I'm waiting for something.

She bucks against my hands, trying to prolong the contact, but I'm not ready for her to come. Not yet. When I move both hands to her tits, her fervor calms a bit, and she seems to concentrate on the sensations—moaning softly. A light sheen of sweat coats her body. It catches the moonlight.

Once she's backed away from the edge, I feel her fingers exploring my pussy, and I allow her to play for a while before returning one of my hands to her sex. I take her back to the edge, then again calm her. Twice. She's writhing and gasping and begging me to let her come, but I'm still not ready.

I hear a small noise and look up to find him leaning against the doorway, watching us. She hasn't noticed, being unable to see and too lost in her own pleasure to hear him.

Now, I'm ready.

"Be still now," I say and wait for her to comply, delivering another slap to her pussy to emphasize my words. "Listen to me. We have company. Are you ready for this?"

About the Authors

Eden Bradley writes erotica and sensual romance in between her duties as book review editor and member liaison at RomanceDivas.com, an award-winning romance writers' resource website, where she has published several articles on writing love scenes.

Eden has been writing since she was old enough to hold a pen. While other children had imaginary friends, she spent her childhood with the characters in her head for company, creating stories for her entertainment. But it was only a few years ago that it occurred to her she should try to actually publish what she was writing. She embarked on the journey to publication, learning everything she could about the craft and business of writing along the way.

When not busy writing, she enjoys a sybaritic life of cooking, eating, gardening, shopping, traveling, lounging and reading everything she can get her hands on. She particularly adores sultry, sensual stories of love. Please visit her website at: www.edenbradleyerotica.com.

* * * *

From the moment **Eliza Gayle** read her first erotic romance novel a couple of years ago, she knew she had found her niche and realized her dream of writing was passing her by. So after years of thinking about it, she finally grabbed her laptop and wrote. These days she likes her stories hot and spicy, whether they be contemporary, fantasy or paranormal, and will write in whatever genre her imagination has conjured that day.
Eliza lives in beautiful North Carolina and spends her days dividing her time between writing, her book video business, a part-time job as promotions manager and raising her two daughters.

* * * *

Reese Gabriel is an internationally known author of erotica, specializing in romance bondage and BDSM. He has over sixty published novels and continues to write at a prolific pace. Reese lives with his wife and best friend of twenty years and enjoys old movies, swimming, and walks on the beach. He is an advocate of human rights and sexual freedom and believes that the best days of the human race are yet to come, as soon as we grow up and learn to live as one species, sanely, and rationally.

* * * *

Alessia Brio is the ultra sexy, erotica-writing alter ego of an Appalachian soccer mom. She is "sensual, succulent, and satisfying" even when her creator feels like a hairy warthog. Her debut book, a single-author anthology of erotica & poetry entitled *fine flickering hungers*, won the 2007 EPPIE Award for Best Erotica.

Alessia is primarily published electronically. She strives to bring a print-level of respectability to ebooks, to promote diversity, and to maintain an altruistic focus in all her efforts. To that end, she is the driving force behind the *Coming Together* anthologies.

Nominated in 2004 as Literotica's Most Influential Poet and in both 2005 & 2006 as its Most Influential Writer, her work also appears online at Oysters & Chocolate, Tit-Elation, Ruthie's Club, The Shadow Sacrament, and Desdmona, where she received honorable mentions in both the Stiletto Flash & Titillating Tattoo erotic writing contests.

When she's not writing, editing, designing covers, or *researching*, Ms. Brio is performing her domestic duties as a work-from-home mom, kicking ass (or kissing it) as a civil rights advocate, or wasting time in cyberspace.

PHAZE SUPPORTS EROTIC ALTRUISM

Printed in the United States
137567LV00001B/5/P